365

Fairy Tales, Rhymes
and Other Stories
for
Girls

Written by: Hettie Bingham, Louise Martin, Aesop, Charles Perrault, Edward Lear, Gaby Goldsack, Brothers Grimm, Hans Christian Andersen, Jan Astly, Jillian Harker, Kath Jewitt, Moira Butterfield, Peter Bently, Rachel Elliott, Rebecca Elliott, Ronne Randall, Sarah Delmege, Monica Hughes, Justine Swain-Smith and Sue Graves.

Illustrated by Dubravka Kolanovic, Jacqueline East and Robert Dunn.

Additional illustrations by Gail Yerrill, Priscilla Lamont, Claire Tindall, Daniel Howarth, Elena Selivanova, Gavin Scott, Gill McLean, Gwyneth Williamson, Kirsteen Harris Jones, Lee Wildish, Lesley Harker, Mei Matsuoka, Paula Bowles, Priscilla Lamont, Shelagh McNicholas, Susan Winter, Steve Lavis, Adrienne Salgado, Gaby Hansen, Andy Catling, Anna Jones, Kerry Timewell, Erica-Jane Waters and Veronica Vasylenko.

Every effort has been made to acknowledge the contributors to this book. If we have made any errors, we will be pleased to rectify them in future editions.

Designed by Blue Sunflower Creative

PRODUCED FOR CHAD VALLEY TOYS
489-499 Avebury Boulevard,
Central Milton Keynes, MK9 2NW

www.argos.co.uk

ISBN 978-1-4454-4629-5
Batch Code: S27868
Made in China

365
Fairy Tales, Rhymes
and Other Stories
for
Girls

Contents

Contents

Contents

Contents

The Gingerbread Man

There was once a little old man and a little old woman. One morning, the old woman decided to bake a gingerbread man. She rolled out the dough and cut out the shape of a little man. She made his eyes, mouth and nose from icing, and gave him three currant buttons. Then she popped him in the oven and baked him until he was golden and crisp. But when the little old woman opened the oven door, the gingerbread man jumped down and ran away.

"Stop!" cried the old woman and man, running after him. But the gingerbread man was too fast for them.

"Run, run as fast as you can.
You can't catch me, I'm the gingerbread man!" he chanted.

The gingerbread man ran past a pig.

"Stop!" snorted the pig. But the gingerbread man ran on.

"Run, run as fast as you can.
You can't catch me, I'm the gingerbread man!" he chanted.

Next the gingerbread man passed a cow.

"Stop!" mooed the cow. But the gingerbread man ran on.

"Run, run as fast as you can.
You can't catch me, I'm the gingerbread man!" he chanted.

Soon he passed a horse.

"Stop!" neighed the horse. But the gingerbread man ran on.

"Run, run as fast as you can.
You can't catch me, I'm the gingerbread man!" he chanted.

After a while, the gingerbread man reached a river and then he had to stop.

"Oh, no! I can't swim," he cried. "How will I get across?"

A sly and hungry fox was waiting nearby.

He saw the gingerbread man and licked his lips.

"Jump onto my tail and I will take you across the river," he told the gingerbread man.

So the gingerbread man jumped onto the fox's tail and the fox began to swim across the river.

"You're too heavy for my tail, jump onto my back," he said. So the gingerbread man jumped onto his back.

After a while, the fox cried, "You're too heavy for my back. Jump onto my nose." So the gingerbread jumped on.

But as soon as they reached the riverbank, the fox flipped the gingerbread man high up into the air, snapped his mouth shut and gobbled him up.

And that was the end of the gingerbread man!

The Frog Prince

Once upon a time there lived a princess who shone with such beauty that even the sun looked dim next to her.

When the weather was hot, the princess would walk through the forest and sit in the shade by a stream. She took a golden ball to play with, and sat by the water, throwing it into the air and catching it. But one day, her hand slipped and the golden ball fell into the water with a **splash!**

The princess sat there and cried, louder and louder until it sounded as if her heart would break. After a while, a warty frog popped his head above the water.

"Why are you crying so?" he asked.

"Because I have dropped my golden ball into the stream and I can't get it back," sobbed the princess.

"What will you give me if I fetch your ball?" croaked the frog.

"I will give you jewels, gold and pearls. If you bring back my golden ball, I will give you anything you want," sniffed the princess through her tears.

But the frog explained that he wasn't interested in treasures. Instead, he wanted the princess's love.

"If you will love me and care for me, be my friend and play with me, let me eat from your plate and sleep on your pillow, then I will fetch back your ball," said the frog.

"Yes. I promise that I will do all of those things," said the princess. But really, she didn't mean what she said.

"He is just a revolting frog," she thought. "He will give back my ball and then I won't do any of those things."

The frog brought back the princess's ball. She took it from him and then ran back to the palace.

That evening, as the royal family sat down to eat, there was a knock at the door. The princess went to see who was there and was horrified to find the frog, who spoke these words:

"Let me in, oh princess sweet,
Don't forget your vow.
Let me be your own dear love.
To your heart, I bow."

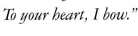

But the princess slammed the door in the frog's face and hurried back to the table.

"Who was that?" asked her father.

"Oh, just a slimy frog," replied the princess. "He would only fetch my ball back for me if I promised to love him. How ridiculous, to think that I should love a warty old frog!"

"A promise is a promise," said the king, who was a fair man. "You must let him in and keep your promise."

And so, much to the princess's dismay, the frog was invited in. The king commanded his daughter to keep her promise and, although she found the frog quite disgusting, she had no choice but to obey her father. The princess allowed the frog to eat from her plate and sleep on her pillow, she even played games with him. But she could not bring herself to care for him or love him. The frog reminded her of the promise she had made to him, saying these words:

"Love me true, oh princess sweet,
Don't forget your vow.
Let me be your own dear love,
You must kiss me now."

But still the princess refused to kiss him.

The frog followed the princess everywhere she went until she became quite angry with him.

"Go away, you horrible beast!" she cried, but the frog stayed by her side night and day.

One day, when the princess was in a particularly bad mood, she picked up the frog and hurled him across the room. He hit the wall and landed on the floor with a bump! He lay there, dazed, and had such a sad expression on his face that the princess felt sorry for what she had done. She rushed over to where he lay, picked him up and kissed him with true compassion.

Suddenly, there was a flash of light and the astonished princess watched on as the frog was transformed into a handsome prince.

"My dear princess," said the prince, falling to his knees. "Please be my wife."

The princess knew for sure that she loved the prince, and that finally her promise was fulfilled. The prince and princess were married in a spectacular ceremony and the bride shone more brightly than the sun. They lived happily ever after.

Seven Ravens

Once there lived a man and a woman who had seven sons, but longed for a daughter. When their eighth child was a girl, they were very happy. At last their wish had come true.

The beautiful baby girl was a thirsty little thing, so the seven sons were sent out to the well to fetch water.

"Take this silver cup and fill it for the baby," said their mother. But the silver cup fell into the well with a splash! The boys were too frightened to go home.

When they didn't return, their father cursed them. "May those lazy good-for-nothing boys become ravens!" he shouted. As soon as the words left his mouth, he saw seven ravens flying off into the distance. Although he regretted his words, it was too late to undo his curse.

When the little girl grew older, her sad mother told her all about her seven lost brothers. The brave girl vowed to find them and bring them home.

She set off, taking her mother's ring as a keepsake, and searched the world over. "Where are my seven brothers?" she called up to the heavens. The stars could see that the poor girl was in despair and took

pity on her. They sent down a magical key and, as the girl picked it up, she heard these words:

"Follow our light to a mountain of glass,
You'll find your raven brothers at last."

After walking for many days, the young girl finally reached the glass mountain. Using the key she entered a crystal cave and, although nobody was there, she noticed seven little plates and cups laid out with food and drink ready for their return.

Being very hungry, she took a bite from each plate and a sip from each cup. Her ring fell into the last cup but, before she could pick it up again, she heard the swish of wings. She hid behind a door and watched seven ravens swoop down.

Each raven noticed that some of their food and drink was missing. Then the last raven found the ring in his cup and recognised it as his mother's.

"If only our little sister has come to find us," he exclaimed, "for then we could return home with her."

On hearing this, their brave little sister jumped out from behind the door. As soon as they saw her, the ravens turned back into their human form.

They returned home to a huge celebration and lived happily ever after.

The Sad Princess

There was once a princess who never laughed.

"Whoever makes my daughter laugh can marry her!" said the king, who didn't know what else to do.

Lots of hopeful young men lined up to try and make the sad princess laugh.

First there was a joke-teller. *"How do you tell which end of a worm is the head? Tickle the middle and see which end laughs!"* he said. But that didn't make the princess laugh. Lots of people tried, but nobody could make the princess laugh.

The king had almost lost hope when he heard a very strange and unusual sound.

"Ha, ha! Hee, hee! Ho, ho!"

He hadn't heard it before, so it took him a while to realise that it was his daughter... **and she was laughing!**

The princess was looking out of the window at a man trying to make his donkey walk. He was pulling the donkey as hard as he could, and still the stubborn donkey would not move at all. The more the donkey refused to move, the more the princess laughed.

And so the princess and the donkey's owner were married, and they lived a happy life together, full of laughter.

A Golden Touch

There was once a king who wished that everything he touched would turn to gold.

His wish was granted by a passing fairy, and he ran around his palace turning all his belongings into gold.

Vases, statues, plates and even cushions were turned to gold as soon as he touched them.

"I will be so **rich**," he thought.

Before long, the king started to feel hungry. "Bring me some fruit," he ordered his servant. But when the king picked up an apple, it turned to gold before it had even reached his lips.

The king began to feel very sad, but when his wife tried to comfort him with a hug, even she turned to gold.

"I **never** want to see gold again," sobbed the king and he wished with all his heart for things to be back to normal.

Luckily, the fairy, who had been watching all along, took pity on him. Everything changed back to the way it had been before.

The king had learned his lesson and he knew that there were many ordinary things more valuable than gold.

The Little Mermaid

Deep beneath the ocean, in a magical watery world, there lived a little mermaid. Although she was very happy under the sea, the little mermaid loved to explore and often swam to the surface, even though her father had told her not to.

One stormy day, the little mermaid swam up to watch the waves splashing against the rocks. She loved the thundery grey clouds and the fresh drops of rainwater that fell upon her face. As she watched from behind a rock, she noticed a ship that was struggling to stay afloat in the stormy waters.

Whoosh! A huge wave hit the ship and sent it crashing against the rocks. The little mermaid watched on helplessly as the fine vessel began to sink.

As the passengers and crew scrambled into the life boats, the little mermaid noticed one very handsome man who was unconscious in the water. Although it was forbidden to be seen by humans, she swam over to him and took him safely to the shore. As the little mermaid waited for the young man to recover, she sang him a beautiful melody. Before long he began to wake up and, as soon as their eyes met, they fell in love.

When the mermaid heard the sound of human voices approaching, she hid behind a rock and watched as some men rushed over to the young man's side.

"Your majesty, thank goodness you're safe," they said. And it was then that the little mermaid realised that her handsome young man was a prince.

Safely back under the sea, the little mermaid could not stop thinking about the prince and she knew she just had to find a way of seeing him again.

In the murky depths, amongst the darkest caves, there lived a sea witch. The little mermaid knew in her heart that the witch was evil, but she wanted to see her prince again so badly that she paid her a visit.

"Poor little heartbroken mermaid," the witch cackled. "I will give you human legs so that you can see your precious prince, but in return I will take your lovely voice! Ha, ha, ha, ha!"

The little mermaid accepted. She would have given anything to be with her true love. Surely he would recognise her, even if she was unable to tell him who she was.

And so the little mermaid swam to the surface, leaving her beautiful voice behind. She collapsed, exhausted, onto the same beach where she had last seen the prince. As luck would have it, the prince was walking on the beach and found her. But although he thought she looked familiar, the prince did not recognise her as the mysterious girl who had saved his life.

"Who are you?" he asked her, but the little mermaid had no words to tell him.

The prince took pity on the strange girl and thought perhaps she might be a survivor from a shipwreck. Although she could not speak, he found her to be a wonderful companion, and grew fonder of her each day.

The little mermaid was happy to be with her prince and thought that he was sure to remember her one day, it would just take time.

But the wicked sea witch was spying on the little mermaid and had become very jealous. It was not enough for her that she had the mermaid's beautiful voice, she wanted the prince for herself, too. She transformed herself into a beautiful woman and set off to meet the prince.

"I am the woman who saved your life," she told the prince, and she entranced him by using the little mermaid's pure young voice, which she kept in a glass bottle around her neck. The prince believed the witch was the girl who had saved him, and he asked her to marry him.

As the palace prepared for a royal wedding, the little mermaid wept bitter tears.

"My heart will break!" she thought to herself as she sobbed.

The day of the wedding arrived and the little mermaid watched on helplessly as the disguised witch walked down the aisle. As she passed the little mermaid she gave her an evil smirk, and was enjoying herself so much that she forgot to watch her step. The witch tripped over her wedding gown and fell. She landed on the bottle, smashing it to smithereens. The mermaid's voice broke free and returned to her.

At once the little mermaid began to sing the same beautiful melody that she had sung on the day she had rescued the prince. The sea witch's magic spell was broken and the prince came to his senses. The sea witch vanished in a puff of smoke and the prince was free to marry his true love. They both lived happily ever after.

Jack and Jill

Jack and Jill went up the hill
To fetch a pail of water;
Jack fell down and broke his crown,
And Jill came tumbling after.
Up Jack got, and home did trot
As fast as he could caper;
He went to bed, to mend his head,
With vinegar and brown paper.

Mrs White

Mrs White had a fright
In the middle of the night;
She saw a ghost, eating toast,
Halfway up a lamppost!

Cobbler, Cobbler

Cobbler, cobbler, mend my shoe,
Get it done by half past two.
Half past two is much too late!
Get it done by half past eight.

Little Miss Muffet

Little Miss Muffet
Sat on a tuffet,
Eating her curds and whey;
Along came a spider,
Who sat down beside her
And frightened Miss Muffet away.

See-Saw, Margery Daw

See-saw, Margery Daw,
Johnny shall have a new master;
He shall have but a penny a day,
Because he can't work any faster.

The Grand Old Duke of York

The grand old Duke of York,
He had ten thousand men,
He marched them up to the top of the hill,
And he marched them down again.
When they were up, they were up,
And when they were down, they were down,
And when they were only half way up,
They were neither up nor down.

Little Brother and Little Sister

Once upon a time, there was a little brother and a little sister who lived with their stepmother who was very cruel to them. One night, the brother and sister decided to run away.

So the two children ran out into the forest, curled up in the hollow of a tree and fell asleep.

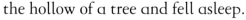

Their stepmother, who was really a wicked **witch**, followed the children. When she found them asleep, she put a curse on a nearby stream knowing that they would drink from it.

The next morning, the two children bent down to drink from the stream. But the stream whispered a warning:

"Brother and sister, although my water's clear, do not drink it, or you'll become a deer." The little sister listened to the warning, but her brother could not resist taking a drink. He was **transformed** into a deer.

"Don't worry, I'll look after you," said the kind sister, and she led the little deer into the woods.

They found a wooden hut in a clearing and, as it was empty, they lived there happily for a long time.

But one spring, a king was hunting in the forest. Thwack! He shot the deer with an arrow. The wounded deer limped back to his sister, now a beautiful woman. The king followed and, when he saw the sister, he lost his heart to her and the two were married. The deer was nursed back to health and stayed with his sister and the king.

After all this time, the brother and sister had almost forgotten about their wicked stepmother, but she had not forgotten them. She knew where they were and still wanted to harm them.

When the king and queen's first child was born, the stepmother crept into the palace grounds to try and steal it. The king's hunting dogs sniffed out the wicked woman and chased her away. They were so fierce that the wicked witch didn't stop running until she had left the kingdom. Once the witch was gone, her spell was broken and the brother returned to his human form.

The witch never bothered them again.

The Princess and the Salt

Once, a rich and powerful king summoned his three daughters to his throne room on his birthday. His first daughter gave him gold, and the second daughter brought him silver. The king was very pleased with these gifts.

"I have brought you salt," said the third daughter.

"**Salt!**" yelled the king. "How dare you insult me? What good is salt?" And he banished his own daughter from his kingdom.

But when the princess left, all the salt in the kingdom vanished. At first, the king complained that his food was tasteless, but then he became very ill from lack of salt.

The king realised how foolish he had been and sent for his daughter. When she returned to the kingdom, the salt also returned.

"Forgive me," said the king. "Your gift of salt was more precious than silver or gold, for you cannot live without salt." From that day on, the king learned to value things other than his riches.

The Straw, the Coal and the Bean

A woman was cooking beans. She lit a fire with some straw and a piece of it fell to the floor. Then she emptied the beans into the cooking pot. Plop! One dropped onto the ground beside the straw. A burning coal leapt down from the fire to join them with a **crackle!**

The straw, the bean and the coal congratulated themselves on escaping the fire which would have destroyed them.

They ran through the open door and didn't stop until they reached a little brook. But there was no bridge over the water, so the straw lay across the brook and invited the others to cross. The coal leapt on first, but half way over he got scared and couldn't move. As he was still hot from the fire, he burned through the straw and they both fell into the water with a hiss!

"Ha, ha, ha!" The bean laughed so hard that she split in two, and that would have been the end of her too, if it wasn't for a tailor who happened to be passing.

The tailor kindly sewed the bean back together again. And that is why, to this very day, some beans have a black seam!

Aladdin

Once upon a time, there was a boy called Aladdin who lived with his poor widowed mother. One evening, a strange man came to visit them.

"I am your long-lost uncle, Abanazar," he told Aladdin. He was not really Aladdin's uncle, but the wicked man knew of a magic lamp hidden in a cave, and he wanted to get his hands on it. The enchanted cave could only be entered by an innocent boy and Abanazar had chosen Aladdin for the job.

Abanazar offered Aladdin a precious ring and gave his mother food, so Aladdin agreed to help.

Abanazar took Aladdin to the cave, and told him the magic words which would open it.

"Open Sesame!" cried Aladdin. The cave opened and it didn't take Aladdin long to find the lamp. But, when he tried to leave the cave, he found that he was trapped. Aladdin rubbed his hands together to keep warm. At the same time, he rubbed the ring Abanazar had given him. There was a puff of smoke and, to his great astonishment, a genie appeared before his very eyes, for the ring was magic.

"What is your wish, oh master?" asked the genie, in a deep booming voice.

"Take me home," said Aladdin, who was still clutching the old lamp. When he got home, he polished the lamp and was amazed to see an even more powerful genie appear.

With the genie's help, Aladdin became so rich and powerful that he was able to marry a princess. But one day, Abanazar came to visit the princess. He offered her a shiny new lamp in exchange for the old one. The princess didn't know about the genie who lived in the lamp, and so she agreed.

Abanazar ran away taking Aladdin's wife with him. Aladdin could not think what to do until he remembered that he still had his old magic ring.

"Help me rescue my wife and get my lamp back," Aladdin commanded the genie of the ring.

The genie and Aladdin rescued the princess and brought back the lamp.

Aladdin was so pleased that he granted both genies their freedom.

Abanazar never troubled Aladdin and his wife again, and they lived happily ever after.

Jack and the Beanstalk

There was once a lazy boy named Jack who lived with his mother. They were very poor indeed. They had no money and nothing left to eat.

"We have no choice but to sell our old cow," said Jack's poor mother. "Take her to market and sell her for the best price you can get."

Jack set off and, before long, he met an old man.

"Where are you off to, lad?" asked the man.

"I'm taking our old cow to market," replied Jack. "If we don't sell her we will starve."

The old man offered to buy the cow right there and then.

"What will you pay me?" asked Jack.

"I will give you these beans," said the old man.

"Beans!" said Jack. "What do you take me for? I'm not a complete fool!"

But the old man explained to Jack that the beans were magic, so thinking that his mother would be pleased, Jack took the beans and handed over the cow.

But his mother was not pleased.

"You **stupid** boy!" she cried. "We can't live on a handful of beans!" She took the beans, threw them out of the window and sent Jack to bed.

The next morning, when Jack woke up, his room seemed darker than usual. He looked out of his window and could hardly believe his eyes when he saw an **enormous beanstalk** that had grown from the beans. It stretched way up into the sky and beyond the clouds. Jack just had to know what was at the top. He started to climb the enormous stalk, pulling himself up bit by bit. It was hard work, but Jack didn't stop and he didn't look down. He **climbed** up through the clouds, and then he climbed some more.

It was a very long time before he reached the top, but eventually Jack found himself in a strange land.

There was a path ahead of him, which he followed. After some time, he reached a **gigantic** castle and knocked on the door. A woman answered.

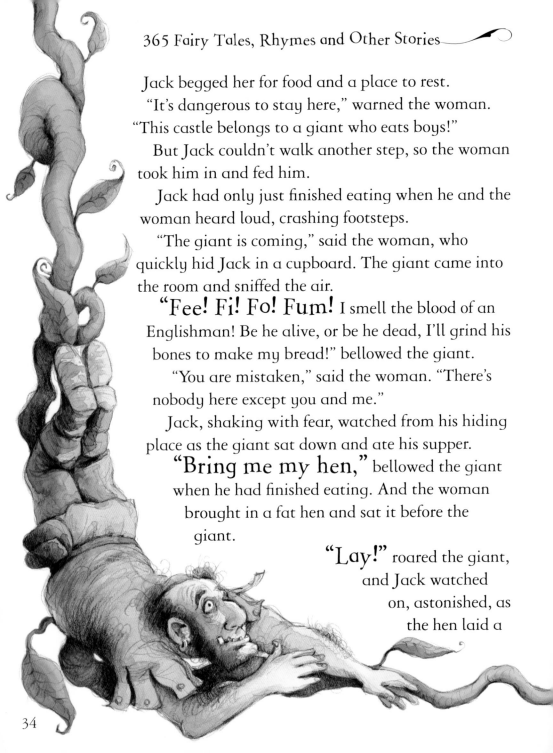

Jack begged her for food and a place to rest.

"It's dangerous to stay here," warned the woman. "This castle belongs to a giant who eats boys!"

But Jack couldn't walk another step, so the woman took him in and fed him.

Jack had only just finished eating when he and the woman heard loud, crashing footsteps.

"The giant is coming," said the woman, who quickly hid Jack in a cupboard. The giant came into the room and sniffed the air.

"Fee! Fi! Fo! Fum! I smell the blood of an Englishman! Be he alive, or be he dead, I'll grind his bones to make my bread!" bellowed the giant.

"You are mistaken," said the woman. "There's nobody here except you and me."

Jack, shaking with fear, watched from his hiding place as the giant sat down and ate his supper.

"Bring me my hen," bellowed the giant when he had finished eating. And the woman brought in a fat hen and sat it before the giant.

"Lay!" roared the giant, and Jack watched on, astonished, as the hen laid a

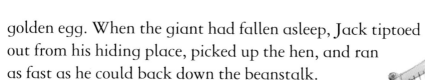

golden egg. When the giant had fallen asleep, Jack tiptoed out from his hiding place, picked up the hen, and ran as fast as he could back down the beanstalk.

When Jack showed his mother how the hen could lay eggs of pure gold, she was delighted.

"We will never be hungry again," she said.

But Jack longed for more adventure and went back up the beanstalk to the castle. He cleverly disguised himself, so the woman agreed to let him in again. Once more, Jack heard the giant approach, and again the woman hid him while the giant sat down to eat.

"Bring me my harp," roared the giant when he had finished eating.

The woman brought in a golden harp which sang to the giant until he fell asleep. Jack crept out from his hiding place and grabbed the harp. But when he ran off, the harp called to his master and the giant woke up. Jack ran for his life with the giant hot on his heels. He climbed back down the beanstalk and the giant followed.

"Mother, fetch the axe!" called Jack when he reached the bottom.

Jack struck at the beanstalk with the axe and it came crashing to the ground, bringing the giant with it. The giant was killed stone dead. Jack and his mother lived a happy and wealthy life from then on.

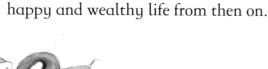

Doctor Foster

Doctor Foster
Went to Gloucester
In a shower of rain;
He stepped in a puddle,
Right up to his middle,
And never went there again!

One Misty, Moisty Morning

One misty, moisty morning,
When cloudy was the weather;
There I met an old man
All clothed in leather.
He began to compliment
And I began to grin;
How do you do?
And how do you do?
And how do you do **again?**

Rain, Rain, Go Away

Rain, rain, go away,
Come again another day.
Little Johnny wants to play.

Rub a Dub Dub

Rub a dub dub,
Three men in a tub,
And how do you think they got there?
The butcher, the baker,
The candlestick maker,
They all jumped out of a rotten potato,
It was enough to make a man stare.

Hector Protector

Hector Protector was dressed all in green;
Hector Protector was sent to the Queen.
The Queen did not like him,
No more did the King;
So Hector Protector was sent back again.

A-Tisket, A-Tasket

A-tisket, a-tasket,
A green and yellow basket.
I wrote a letter to my love,
And on the way I dropped it.
I dropped it, I dropped it,
And on the way I dropped it.
A little boy picked it up,
And put it in his pocket.

Thumbelina

There was once an old woman who wanted a daughter more than anything else in the world.

She went to see a witch who gave her a seed to plant. The seed grew into a beautiful flower and when the flower opened with a pop! a tiny little girl was sitting in the middle. The girl was no bigger than the woman's thumb, so she called her Thumbelina and loved her like a daughter.

The woman gave Thumbelina a walnut shell to sleep in and made sure she had everything she wanted. Thumbelina was very happy living with her mother.

One night, an old toad-woman passed by an open window. Hop, hoppity, hop! She saw Thumbelina as she lay asleep in her walnut shell.

"What a tiny girl," she thought to herself. "She would make a lovely bride for my son." And the toad-woman carried Thumbelina away.

Poor Thumbelina was horrified when she woke up and saw a big warty face staring at her.

"Who are you?" she gasped.

"I am Toad, and you will be my wife," said the ugly creature. And he hopped off, leaving Thumbelina stranded on a lily pad, while he and his mother set to work preparing the wedding.

Thumbelina could think of nothing worse than being married to a toad. She wept bitter tears, which fell into the river with a **splash!**

Some fish swam up to the surface, thinking the tear drops were insects that they could eat. When they saw the tiny girl crying her heart out, the fish took pity on her.

"Sniff! If I can't escape from here, I'll have to marry a toad," sobbed Thumbelina. The helpful fish nibbled through the stem of the lily pad, and Thumbelina floated away down the river.

The lily pad landed on a river bank near a corn field, and Thumbelina clambered off. She felt all alone in the world and began to weep again. A field-mouse scuttled past and stopped to see what was the matter.

"I am far from home," sobbed Thumbelina. "I have nobody to care for me."

The field-mouse felt very sorry for Thumbelina. He could not leave such a pretty creature crying and alone.

"Come and live with me, I'll look after you," he offered.

So Thumbelina lived underground where she was safe and warm. The field-mouse was very kind to her and they spent many happy days together.

The field-mouse's best friend was a mole, and he grew so fond of Thumbelina that he wanted to marry her. But the thought of living underground for the rest of her life made Thumbelina sad. She missed the open air and sunshine.

One day, as Thumbelina was walking through an underground passage, she saw a swallow. There seemed to be no life in the poor creature and, thinking he had died from cold, she wrapped him up.

But the bird wasn't dead. When he had warmed up he began to stir with a **flitter, flutter!** The swallow was very grateful to Thumbelina and wanted to help her.

"Come away with me," said the swallow. "We can fly off to a warmer land."

Thumbelina climbed onto the swallow's back, and together they flew over the bleak winter landscape until they noticed that the air was getting warmer and the land was becoming greener.

The swallow swooped down into a meadow full of flowers. Thumbelina thought it was the most beautiful place she had ever seen. The ground was thick with colourful blooms and the air was full of birds singing. The sun shone

all day long and Thumbelina felt warm and happy.

"I would like to stay here," she said. So the swallow landed, and Thumbelina jumped down from his back.

Thumbelina climbed into a lovely pink flower and breathed in its heady scent. As she looked around the meadow, she noticed that each of the flowers had a tiny sprite living in it. They were just like Thumbelina, and she felt as if she were home at last.

The king of the flower sprites flew to Thumbelina and welcomed her. When he saw Thumbelina's happy face, he fell in love and asked her to marry him. Thumbelina agreed, and they had a beautiful wedding, filled with flowers and sunshine.

Thumbelina became the queen of the flower sprites, and lived happily ever after.

Mother Hulda

There was once a woman with two daughters. Her stepdaughter was hard working and beautiful while her own daughter was ugly and lazy. The woman preferred her own daughter, and made her stepdaughter do all the work around the house.

One day, the woman gave her stepdaughter an enormous basket of wool.

"Take this wool and spin it all. Don't come back until it's finished," she told her.

So the stepdaughter sat and span until her fingers bled. She went to wash her fingers in the well, but accidently dropped the spindle into the water. Plop!

She climbed down to find it and, when she reached the bottom of the well, she found herself in a strange land. After walking a while she reached a little house. A kind woman called Mother Hulda lived there and gave the girl food and shelter. In return, the girl helped Mother Hulda with all her chores.

But after a while, even though this woman was so much

kinder than her stepmother, she began to feel homesick. "I would like to return home," said the girl to Mother Hulda.

So Mother Hulda gave the girl back her spindle and, as the girl left the strange land, a **shower of gold** fell down and stuck to her.

When the girl arrived home, her stepmother was amazed. She wanted the same thing to happen to her own lazy daughter.

"Do just as your sister did," she told the lazy girl. But the lazy daughter could not be bothered to sit and spin, so she stuck her hands into a thorny bush to make them bleed. Then she dropped the spindle down the well and climbed in after it.

The lazy girl knocked on Mother Hulda's door and asked for food and shelter. She ate her fill and then fell asleep, **snoring** like a pig!

"Give me back my spindle. I want to go home now," said the rude girl to Mother Hulda when she woke up.

So Mother Hulda took the girl back to the bottom of the well. But instead of gold, it was **tar** that fell upon her.

The lazy girl returned to her mother who tried to scrub her clean. But the tar was stuck fast, and remained so for the rest of her life.

The Fisherman
and his Wife

One day, when the sea was blue and calm, a poor fisherman set off to work. At first he caught nothing and was about to call it a day, when he felt a tug on his line. His catch pulled hard as he struggled to wind it in. "This must be a very big fish," he thought. The fish was enormous, and the fisherman was very pleased. But his pleasure turned to astonishment when the fish spoke to him.

"Please throw me back," pleaded the fish. "I am not really a fish at all, but an **enchanted prince.**"

The stunned fisherman put the fish back into the water and set off for home.

The fisherman and his wife were so poor that they lived in a pigsty. When he told his wife about the talking fish she was angry with him.

"**You fool!**" she said. "No wonder that we're so poor if you can't see a good thing when it's biting you on the nose!"

The fisherman's wife told him that, if the fish was an enchanted prince, he should have asked for something in return for setting him free.

"Go back to the same spot tomorrow and catch that fish again, and this time ask him for a little cottage so we can live a better life," said the fisherman's wife.

The next morning, when the sea was green and choppy, the fisherman set off again. He rowed out to the same spot as the day before, hoping to see the magical fish.

"Enchanted prince, please hear my plea, jump out from the water and talk to me," called the fisherman.

The fish appeared and asked the fisherman why he had called him. The fisherman explained that he was a very poor man and would like to live in a little cottage instead of a pigsty.

"Go home," said the fish. "Your wish is granted." And he left with a
splish!

So the fisherman returned to his wife, who waved to him from the window of their lovely new cottage.

The fisherman's wife was happy for a little while, but soon became discontented again.

"I think we could have asked for more from that magic

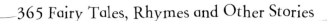

fish," she told her husband one evening. "This is only a small cottage, a castle would be much better." And she begged her husband to go and find the magic fish, and ask him to grant her wish.

The next morning, when the sea was purple and rough, the fisherman set off again and rowed out to the same spot as before.

"Enchanted prince, please hear my plea, jump out from the water and talk to me," called the fisherman.

The fish appeared, although he didn't seem very happy about being called again. The fisherman explained that his wife found the cottage rather small, and would prefer to live in a castle.

"Go home," said the fish. "Your wish is granted." And he left with a **splash!**

So the fisherman returned to his wife, who waved to him from the window of a grand castle.

But the fisherman's wife wanted even more. "If that fish can give us a grand castle, he can make me a queen," she said.

The next morning, when the sea was grey and smelly, the fisherman set off again and rowed out to the same spot as before. *"Enchanted prince, please hear my plea, jump out from the water and talk to me,"* called the fisherman.

The fish appeared, not at all pleased to be called again. The fisherman explained that his wife now wanted to be a queen.

"Go home," said the fish. "Your wish is granted." And he left with a splosh!

So the fisherman returned to his wife, who was now a queen.

"If that fish can make me a queen, then he can make me the ruler of the whole world!" said the fisherman's wife.

The next morning, when the sea was black and stormy, the fisherman set off again and rowed out to the same spot as before. *"Enchanted prince, please hear my plea, jump out from the water and talk to me,"* called the fisherman.

The fish appeared, and he was furious. The fisherman explained that his wife now wanted to be the ruler of the world. "Go home," said the fish. "Your wife has what she deserves." And he left with a splish! splash! splosh!

So the fisherman returned to his wife... who was living in the pigsty again!

The Snow Queen

Once upon a time, there was a wicked elf who made a magic mirror that showed everything in a bad light. When the mirror broke with a **crack!** hundreds of glass shards went flying out around the world.

Kai and Gerda were a little girl and boy who had grown up with each other and were like brother and sister.

One day, when they were playing outside, a shard of the broken mirror lodged in Kai's eye. Kai became very cold and unfriendly, and poor Gerda had no idea what had happened to him.

"Come and play with me, Kai," begged Gerda. She hoped that Kai would come to his senses and be friendly again. But Kai was **bitterly cold** to her, and all around him.

"I don't want to play with you any more. Leave me alone," he said.

Kai liked the cold and the ice. Snowflakes became his favourite thing of all. He spent all day looking at

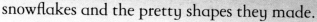

snowflakes and the pretty shapes they made.

Before long, the Snow Queen herself came to notice Kai, and one day she came to see him. "I can take you to a place where it is always cold and snowy," she told Kai. And so Kai went away with her.

Nobody knew where Kai had gone, and most people thought that he must be dead. But Gerda felt in her heart that he was still alive. She never lost faith in her old friend and vowed to find him.

Gerda set of to look for Kai wearing new red shoes. After a while she came to a river. "River, have you seen my friend Kai?" she asked. But the river would not reply. So Gerda removed her lovely red shoes, and offered them to the river.

"I will give you these new red shoes if you will help me find my friend," she told the river, and threw the shoes into the water with a **splash!** The river replied:

"In my murky waters deep, many secrets do I keep.
But no boy rested his head upon my muddy river bed."

Gerda was relieved to find out that Kai had not drowned, and set off again. She walked for many miles until she came to a beautiful garden where she stopped to rest.

Gerda lay down amongst the fragrant flowers, and fell asleep.

She dreamed of flowers pushing up through the soil.

When she woke up, she thought she could hear the flowers whispering to her. She listened carefully and, sure enough, a beautiful rose spoke to her:

"Beneath the ground where roots run deep,
I cannot see your friend asleep."

Gerda was happy because she knew this meant that Kai wasn't dead. She set off once more to look for her dear friend.

While Gerda was walking through a forest, she met a reindeer.

"Reindeer, have you seen my friend Kai?" she asked him.

"Is he the boy who likes snowflakes?" replied the reindeer.

"Yes, they are his favourite thing," said Gerda.

The kind reindeer told Gerda that he had seen Kai in the grounds of the Snow Queen's palace. "Climb onto my back, and I'll take you there," he said. Gerda thought her heart would burst with happiness. She felt sure that she would soon find Kai and take him home.

But when she and the reindeer reached the Snow Queen's land, they found that it was guarded by snowflakes.

"How will we ever get past these snowflakes?" thought Gerda. But as she walked through them, they were melted by the warmth of her heart. Gerda and the reindeer walked through the icy land searching everywhere for Kai.

"There he is!" said Gerda, suddenly, seeing her old friend sitting in the middle of a frozen lake. She rushed over to greet him, but when she flung her arms around him, she was heartbroken to realise that Kai did not remember who she was.

"Who are you?" said Kai. "Leave me alone." But Gerda would not let go of him. She cried so hard that Kai's icy heart began to melt. Kai started crying as well, and his own tears washed the shard of broken mirror from his eye.

"Gerda, is it really you?" asked Kai.

"Yes. I've come to take you home," said Gerda. But Kai noticed the Snow Queen riding towards them. "We must leave this place quickly," warned Kai. "The Snow Queen will freeze our hearts and make us stay here." So Kai and Gerda climbed onto the reindeer's back and rode away from the icy land. They were never parted again and lived happily ever after.

There Was an Old Woman

There was an old woman who lived in a shoe.
She had so many children she didn't know what to do!
So she gave them some broth without any bread,
And she told them off
soundly and sent them to bed.

Monday's Child

Monday's child is fair of face,
Tuesday's child is full of grace,
Wednesday's child is full of woe,
Thursday's child has far to go,
Friday's child is loving and giving,
Saturday's child works hard for his living,
And the child that is born on the Sabbath day
Is bonny and blithe and good and gay.

Each Peach, Pear, Plum

Each peach, pear, plum, out goes Tom Thumb;
Tom Thumb won't do, out goes Betty Blue;
Betty Blue won't go, so out goes you.

Old King Cole

Old King Cole was a merry old soul,
And a merry old soul was he;
He called for his pipe in the middle of the night,
And he called for his fiddlers three.

Every fiddler had a very fine fiddle,
and a very fine fiddle had he;
Oh there's none so rare as can compare,
With King Cole and his fiddlers three.

Ip Dip

Ip dip, sky blue.
Who's it? Not you.
Not because you're dirty,
Not because you're clean,
My mother says you're the fairy queen.

Tom, Tom, the Piper's Son

Tom, Tom, the piper's son,
Stole a pig and away he ran.
The pig was eat, and Tom was beat,
And Tom went roaring down the street.

The Wolf and the Seven Young Kids

An old mother goat lived with her seven little kids. One day she went out and left them alone, warning them that the wolf might come, and they must not let him in.

"Don't let that rascal trick you," she said. "He has a gruff old voice and his paws are as black as coal. That is how you will recognise him."

Sure enough, not long after the mother goat had left, there was a knock, knock, knock! at the door.

"Let me in," said a gruff old voice.

"We know it's you, wolf," said the kids. "You have such a gruff old voice."

So the wolf went away and ate some chalk to soften his voice. Then he went back to the goats' house and knocked on the door.

"Let me in," he said with his smooth, chalky voice. But the seven young kids noticed his black paws peeping through a crack in the bottom of the door. "We know it's you, wolf," said the kids. "Your paws are as black as coal."

So the wolf went away and covered his paws with white flour. Then he went back to the goats' house and knocked on the door.

"Let me in," he said. His voice was not gruff and

his paws were not black, so the seven young kids opened the door and let him in.

Gulp! The wolf ate six young kids, but the seventh young kid hid in a cupboard.

When the mother goat returned home, the seventh kid ran out from the cupboard and told her all about the wolf.

"Oh, my poor babies!" cried the mother goat. "We must go and find that wicked wolf." And they set off to look for him.

They found the old rascal sleeping beneath a tree. The mother goat carefully cut open the wolf's big fat stomach with a snip, snip! and six young kids hopped out alive and well!

Then she picked up six stones and put them in the wolf's stomach before sewing it back up again.

They all hid behind a tree and watched.

The wolf woke up feeling thirsty and went to get some water from the well. But the weight of the stones made him fall down the well, and he landed in the water with a splash! And he was never seen again.

The mother goat and her kids danced all the way home!

The Three Little Men

There was once a girl called Helena who lived with her father, stepmother and stepsister, Demona. Helena was kind and beautiful, but Demona was unpleasant and ugly.

The stepmother was an evil woman and vowed to get rid of Helena. "Go and gather strawberries, and don't come back without them," she told Helena one cold day.

The evil stepmother sent Helena out wearing only a paper dress and with just one crust of bread. Helena searched for many hours, but it was far too cold for strawberries to grow.

After a while she came to a little cottage. Feeling very cold, she knocked on the door. Three little men lived there and they let her in to sit by the fire.

"Why are you out in the cold wearing only a paper dress?" asked the men.

"My stepmother made me wear it. She has sent me to find wild strawberries," replied Helena.

Helena shared her small crust of bread with the three little men, although it was all she had. The three little men asked Helena to sweep the leaves from their path. As Helena swept, the three little men decided to give her magic gifts, to reward her for her help.

"She shall become more **beautiful** every day," said the first little man.

"When she speaks, **gold coins** will fall from her mouth," said the second little man.

"She will marry a **king**," said the third little man.

As Helena swept the path, she noticed some wild strawberries. She filled her basket and returned home.

When the stepmother saw Helena's good fortune, she sent Demona to the cottage. But instead of a paper dress, she wore a fur coat. And instead of bread, she took a fine lunch.

Once at the cottage, Demona sat by the fire, eating her fine lunch, without sharing it. When the three little men asked Demona to sweep their path, she refused.

When the rude girl had left them, the three little men decided to give Demona some magic gifts.

"She shall become more **ugly** every day," said the first little man.

"Each time she speaks, a **toad** will jump from her mouth," said the second little man.

"She will live an **unhappy** life," said the third little man.

The magic gifts all came true. Helena married a king and lived happily ever after. Demona did not.

Tom Thumb

There was once a poor couple who had no children and longed for a son of their own.

One day, an old beggar man passed by their house. Although the poor couple had little enough for themselves, they invited him in to eat and rest.

"Where are your children?" asked the beggar.

"We don't have any," sighed the man. We would dearly love a son, even if he were no bigger than my thumb."

Little did the unhappy couple realise that their guest had magical powers. He rewarded their kindness by granting their wish to have a son, even a very tiny one.

The next morning, when the couple came downstairs to breakfast, they found a tiny boy waiting for them on the table. He was no bigger than the man's thumb, and so his delighted parents named him Tom Thumb.

Tom had an unstoppable sense of adventure. "You are only small and the world is a dangerous place," warned his mother. But Tom was too busy having fun to listen.

One day, Tom was

playing by the river. He fell in and got eaten by a fish. The fish was caught and taken to the king's chef. Being a quick-thinking lad, Tom managed to crawl out of the fish. The chef was very shocked to see a tiny boy climbing out from the king's dinner!

Thinking the chef might harm him, Tom ran away. He hid in a mouse hole and soon made friends with the mouse who lived there.

"Climb onto my back," said the mouse. And Tom rode through the palace on the mouse's back, until he found himself in the throne room.

"My goodness!" exclaimed the king. "What have we here?"

Tom sang a song and danced for the king, who was delighted with the tiny boy and asked him to come and live at the palace.

When the king heard that Tom had parents who would be missing him, he sent for the poor couple and let them live in a cottage of their own in the royal grounds.

Tom entertained the king and all his courtiers, and he could visit his parents whenever he liked.

Tom and his parents lived happily ever after.

The Farmer's in his Den

The farmer's in his den,
The farmer's in his den,
Ee-i-addio!
The farmer's in his den.

The farmer wants a wife,
The farmer wants a wife,
Ee-i-addio!
The farmer wants a wife.

The wife wants a child,
The wife wants a child,
Ee-i-addio!
The wife wants a child.

The House that Jack Built

This is the house that Jack built.

This is the malt
That lay in the house that Jack built.

This is the rat,
That ate the malt
That lay in the house that Jack built.

This is the cat,
That killed the rat that ate the malt
That lay in the house that Jack built.

This is the dog,
That worried the cat,
That killed the rat,
That ate the malt
That lay in the house that Jack built.

This is the cow with the crumpled horn,
That tossed the dog, that worried the cat,
That killed the rat, that ate the malt
That lay in the house that Jack built.

The Worn-out Dancing Shoes

There was once a king with twelve beautiful daughters.

Every morning the princesses' dancing shoes were worn right through and the king did not know why. He promised the hand in marriage of one of his daughters to any man who could solve the mystery. Many men tried and failed.

One day, a wounded soldier was walking through the kingdom. He met an old woman who told him about the princesses and said that he should try to solve the puzzle.

"When the princesses bid you goodnight, they will bring you a glass of wine. It is a sleeping potion and you must not drink it," warned the old woman. She also gave him a magic cloak that would make him invisible.

The soldier arrived at the palace and was shown to a bedroom next door to the twelve princesses. When the princesses came to say goodnight, they gave him a glass of wine, but he didn't drink it. He put on his cloak and became invisible, just in time to see the princesses disappearing down through the floor and into a secret passage.

The soldier followed them to a lake where he saw twelve princes, each waiting in a rowing boat. The princesses climbed aboard and the soldier jumped in behind the youngest.

"The boat feels heavy tonight," remarked the prince.

On the other side of the lake was a beautiful land. The trees were made of silver and jewels. The soldier took a twig to take back to the king. When he snapped off the twig, it made a **cracking** sound.

"What was that noise?" asked a prince. But nobody else had heard.

The princesses and princes soon reached a hall, where there was music playing, and they began to dance. The soldier joined in, but he was clumsy and trod on one of the princesses' toes.

"**Ow!** How clumsy you are tonight," she said to her prince. The dancing continued until dawn, when they returned home. The soldier noticed that the princesses had worn out their dancing shoes yet again.

At breakfast, the soldier showed the king the silver twig and explained what had happened. The princesses could not deny the truth and so the mystery was solved.

The soldier married the oldest princess, who was anyway rather tired of dancing, and they lived happily ever after.

Walking in the Woods

If you hear a growl whilst walking in the woods,
It could be Mister Wolf looking for some food.
So never stop and linger, because I've got this hunch,
If you don't keep walking you could end up as...lunch!

The woods are very nice to stroll through when it's sunny.
But if you meet a wolf, you won't think it so funny!
His great big teeth are sharp, he has little else to do
Than to hide behind a tree and wait to pounce on...you!

Knights in Armour

In days gone by, or so I'm told,
The knights were **brave** and very bold.
They galloped over hill and dale,
And rescued maidens, fair and pale,
From very dangerous situations –
They were the **heroes** of the nation!

In armoured suits they went on quests,
(Of course, beneath they wore their vests),
And fought in battles far away,
From early morn 'til close of day.
And when the knights returned victorious,
Their welcome home was always **glorious!**

Coffee and Tea

Molly, my sister, and I fell out,
And what do you think it was all about?
She loved coffee and I loved tea,
And that was the reason we couldn't agree.

There Was a Little Girl

There was a little girl,
And she had a little curl,
Right in the middle
Of her forehead.

When she was good,
She was very, very good,
But when she was bad,
She was **horrid**.

Lavender's Blue

Lavender's blue, dilly, dilly,
Lavender's green;
When I am king, dilly, dilly,
You shall be queen.

Polly, Put the Kettle On

Polly, put the kettle on,
Polly, put the kettle on,
Polly, put the kettle on,
We'll all have tea.
Sukey, take it off again,
Sukey, take it off again,
Sukey, take it off again,
They've all gone away.

Lucy Locket

Lucy Locket lost her pocket,
Kitty Fisher found it,
Not a penny was there in it,
Only ribbon round it.

Mary, Mary, Quite Contrary

Mary, Mary, quite contrary,
How does your garden grow?
With silver bells and cockle shells
And pretty maids all in a row.

The Valiant Little Tailor

A little tailor was taking a break from his work to eat some bread and jam when he noticed flies buzzing around it. In a fury he swatted the flies and counted seven bodies. Feeling very pleased with himself, he carefully stitched onto his belt the words 'seven in one blow' and went out to show off.

The tailor put some cheese in his pocket and, as he walked out, he saw a little bird and put that in his pocket as well.

By and by, the little tailor saw a giant. Feeling brave and fearless he went and talked to him. "Hello there," he called.

"What do you want with me, you little pipsqueak?" roared the giant. The tailor showed his belt to the giant, who thought it meant he had killed seven *men* in one blow.

The giant picked up a rock and squeezed it until water dripped out. "I bet you can't do that," he said.

"No problem," replied the little tailor, and he picked the cheese out of his pocket and squeezed it until water came dripping out.

The giant was fooled by this and took another rock, this time throwing it way into the air. "I bet you can't throw a rock as high as that," he said.

The tailor picked the bird from his pocket and

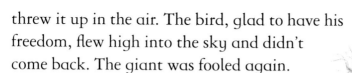

threw it up in the air. The bird, glad to have his freedom, flew high into the sky and didn't come back. The giant was fooled again.

Word soon spread that the little tailor was **amazingly strong.** The king came to hear about it and asked to see the little tailor. He told the tailor about two terrible giants that lived in his woods. "If you defeat the two **monstrous** giants, you can marry my daughter," said the king.

The valiant little tailor found the two giants asleep under a tree. He climbed the tree and began to drop rocks onto one of them. The second giant woke up and accused the first giant of throwing rocks. The first giant said that it wasn't him, and the two giants went back to sleep. Then the tailor threw rocks at the second giant, who woke up in a rage. The two giants fought each other until they both fell down dead.

Everyone believed that the tailor had killed the giants himself, and he became a hero. He married the king's daughter and lived happily ever after, with nobody ever doubting the words on his belt!

The Three Little Pigs

Once upon a time, there were three little pigs who set off to build houses of their own.

After a while the pigs passed a farmer carrying some straw. "Please may I have some of your straw?" asked the first little pig. The farmer agreed, and so the first little pig built his house from **straw.**

Meanwhile, the other two little pigs had walked on and found some sticks. "I will build my house with **sticks,**" said the second little pig.

The third little pig, who was the cleverest of the three, decided that he would build his house from **bricks.**

The three little pigs all settled into their new houses. But it wasn't long before a big bad wolf **sniffed** them out.

The big bad wolf went to the house of straw and knocked on

the door. "Little pig, little pig, let me come in," he called.

"Not by the hair on my chinny, chin, chin," replied the first little pig. So the wolf **huffed** and he **puffed,** and he blew the house in! The first little pig ran to his brother's house of twigs. But the wolf followed and knocked on the door.

"Little pigs, little pigs, let me come in," he called.

Not by the hair on our chinny, chin, chins," replied the pigs. So the wolf **huffed** and he **puffed** and he blew the house in. So the little pigs ran off to the house of the third little pig which was built from bricks.

But the wolf followed and he knocked on the door.

"Little pigs, little pigs, let me come in," he called.

"Not by the hair on our chinny, chin, chins," replied the pigs. So the wolf **huffed** and he **puffed,** and he **huffed** and he **puffed,** but he could not blow the house down.

"Ha, ha!" said the third little pig. "My house is too strong for you to blow down!"

But the wolf was not ready to give up and he started to climb onto the roof. The pigs knew that he planned to climb down the chimney and put a big pot of water to boil in the fireplace. When the wolf climbed down the chimney, he landed with a **splash!** And that was the end of the big bad wolf!

The Pied Piper of Hamelin

The town of Hamelin was overrun by rats.

One day, a stranger came to see the mayor. "I will rid your town of rats if you pay me one hundred gold coins," he said.

The mayor agreed and so the stranger began to play an enchanting tune on a pipe. The rats followed the piper, who led them into a river where they drowned. But when the piper went to ask for his money, the mayor refused to pay.

The next day, the piper returned and played his tune again. This time it was not rats that followed him, but children. "When you pay me what you owe, I will return the children," he told the mayor.

The people of Hamelin were **furious.** They all marched to the town hall to see the mayor.

"Pay the piper what he is owed," they shouted.

The mayor paid the piper, and the children were returned to their parents.

The people of Hamelin chose a new mayor and, from then on, Hamelin thrived.

The Singing Tree

A prince sat to rest beneath a cherry tree, which was covered in white blossom, and fell asleep.

The prince dreamed that the tree was singing:
"Through the dark forest, beyond blue trees,
Follow a path leading down to the sea.
Walk on the beach with red sand at low tide,
And you'll find a true-love to be your bride."

When the prince woke up, he was covered in white blossom. Remembering the words that the tree had sung to him, he set off through the dark forest.

After walking for a day and a night, he came to a cluster of blue trees. Beyond the trees, a winding path led to a beach.

He watched as the tide went out, revealing red sand. Walking along the red sand, he noticed some steps, which he climbed. At the top of the steps, he found himself in the grounds of a grand palace. And there sitting on the grass was his true love.

They were married under the cherry tree, and used its blossom as confetti.

The Wedding of Mrs Fox

Mrs Fox was feeling very sad because her husband had died.

"Don't be so sad," said her maid, who was a cat. "You'll soon find someone else to marry." But Mrs Fox wasn't so sure.

"I'll never find another husband as good as Mr Fox," she sighed. "He had such fine **red stockings** and such a lovely **pointed mouth.**"

One day, the maid knocked on Mrs Fox's door.

"Here's Mr Badger to see you," she said. And in came Mr Badger. Mrs Fox could not deny that he had lovely black and white stripes, but he did not have fine red stockings or a lovely pointed mouth. So, when he asked Mrs Fox to be his wife, she turned him down.

One day, the maid knocked on Mrs Fox's door again. "Here's Mr. Squirrel to see you," she said. And in came Mr Squirrel.

Mrs Fox admired Mr Squirrel's lovely bushy tail, but he did not have fine red stockings or a lovely pointed mouth. So when he begged her to marry him, Mrs Fox said that

she would rather not.

One day, the maid knocked on Mrs Fox's door yet again. "Here's Mr Mouse to see you," she said. And in came Mr Mouse.

"Mrs Fox had to admit that he did have a rather attractive pointed mouth, but no fine red stockings. So when he popped the question, Mrs Fox was flattered, but still refused him.

One day, the maid knocked on Mrs Fox's door yet again. "There's a young man to see you," she said. And in came a handsome fox. He had a beautiful pointed mouth, and very fine red stockings. The handsome fox came to visit Mrs Fox every day, and they fell in love.

"Mrs Fox, will you be my bride?" asked the handsome fox.

"Yes!" replied Mrs Fox. And they lived happily ever after.

The Cockerel King

There was once a very boastful king who would show off at the slightest opportunity. If he had a new robe, he would strut around the palace showing it off. "Look at my fine new robe. It's made of the finest silk and fur," he would say.

"Look at you, **strutting** around just like a cockerel," his wife would think.

One day, a pedlar came to the palace to sell his wares. "Here's just the thing for such a fine fellow as you," the pedlar told the king, as he showed him a carved wooden mirror.

The king bought the mirror and went to sit on his throne to look at himself. But he didn't know that the mirror was a magic one. When he looked into it, he was surprised to see a proud **cockerel** staring back at him.

"This is outrageous," the king thought to himself, "I demand a refund!" But when he tried to get down from his throne, he found that he was no longer a man, but a fine feathered cockerel.

Just then, his butler came in and saw a cockerel strutting around, so he chased it outside. The king tried to protest, but his words came out as a loud **cock-a-doodle doo!**

Outside the palace, the cockerel king began to crow, and he did not stop

until his wife looked out of the window.

"Be quiet, you old cockerel," she called down to him. "Isn't it enough that I have to listen to my boastful husband crowing all day long without your dreadful noise?"

The cockerel king at once fell silent. He hadn't realized what the queen had thought of him until that very moment.

"I suppose I am rather a show-off," he thought sadly to himself. "I will change my ways if only I can be a man again."

Suddenly, there was a flash of light and the king was himself once more. He went back to the throne room and carefully picked up the mirror without looking at himself, and locked it safely away. The king did change his ways from then on and was careful not to boast or show-off too much, but he never dared to look in the magic mirror again – just in case!

The Six Swans

Once upon a time, there was a king with six sons and one daughter.

The king had recently married, but his new wife was a wicked woman and was very **jealous** of his children. One day, in a jealous rage, she turned the king's six sons into swans. The six swans flew away leaving the daughter behind.

The daughter was very upset and she vowed to find her brothers.

She set off and searched for many days throughout the kingdom, until at last she found them living in a little house in the woods.

The six swans told their sister that, to set them free, she must stay **completely silent** for six years and spend that time sewing them each a shirt made from star flowers.

It was no easy task to sew shirts from flowers, and the girl stayed in the woods stitching them for a very long time.

After a few years, a king came riding through the woods and saw the girl as she sat working. Although she wouldn't utter a single word, or even laugh, he fell in love with her gentle nature and sweet smile, and they were married.

The king's mother was jealous

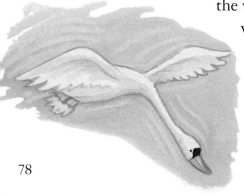

of his new queen's pretty face. She was consumed with hatred and plotted to get rid of her.

Before long, the girl had a baby. The king's mother took the baby away and hid it. Then the evil woman accused the queen of killing it. But the queen was determined to keep her promise to her brothers and would not speak, even to defend herself. So her husband ordered that she be locked away.

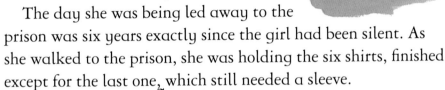

The day she was being led away to the prison was six years exactly since the girl had been silent. As she walked to the prison, she was holding the six shirts, finished except for the last one, which still needed a sleeve.

The girl heard the **flapping** of wings. Six swans flew down to her and she knew they were her brothers. She threw a shirt to each swan and, as she did so, each one returned to their human form, although the last brother had one wing where an arm should be. Finally, the girl could speak again. She told her husband everything that had happened, and the baby was found where the king's mother had hidden it.

The king **banished** his mother forever, and from that day on, they all lived happily ever after.

The White Snake

There was once a king who ate a secret dish every day. One day the king's servant peeked beneath the cover of the secret dish. He was amazed to see that it was a white snake, and he tasted some. Eating the white snake gave him a **magical power** to understand animals.

The servant went to seek his fortune and listen to what the animals had to say.

As he sat by a river one day, he saw that three fish had become entangled in the water reeds.

"**Help!** We will die if we can't get ourselves free," said the fish. The servant heard them and set them free.

As the servant walked on, he saw three baby ravens who had fallen from their nest.

"Who will help us to get food now?" they said. But the servant heard them talking and he shared his food with them.

One day, the servant entered a kingdom where the king had promised that any man who could complete a difficult task could marry his daughter. Many had died trying, but the servant thought he would have a go.

The king threw a **golden ring** deep into a stormy sea and told the servant to retrieve it. The servant began to swim out into the waves. Before long, the three fish swam up to him with the ring.

"One good turn deserves another," said the fish. So the task was completed and the king told the servant that he could marry his daughter.

The daughter, however, didn't want to marry a lowly servant. "Find the golden apple from the tree of life, and bring it to me. Then I will marry you," said the princess.

The servant walked for many days but he couldn't find the **tree of life.** The three ravens, now grown, came to help. They flew off and soon returned with the golden apple.

The servant took the apple to his princess. They shared the delicious fruit and, as each of them took a bite, they fell in love.

They were married that spring, and the servant could hear the animals talking.

"What a lovely couple!" they all said.

The Magic Pear

Once upon a time, a farmer's daughter looked up at an old pear tree and noticed that one pear on the tree was different from all the others. It was larger and had a golden tone to it. She wanted to eat it but it was too high to reach.

As she gazed hungrily up at the unusual pear, a gust of wind blew it down to her. She bit into the golden fruit and it tasted more delicious than any pear she had ever tasted.

As she swallowed the first bite, a **strange** thing happened. The girl saw a vision of herself, and she was dressed as a queen. She laughed at such a ridiculous idea. How could a farmer's daughter become a **queen?**

The next day, a handsome man rode by her farm, and he fell off his horse. The farmer's daughter looked after him until he had fully recovered. During the time she spent nursing him, they fell in love.

"Come back to my palace and be my queen," said the handsome man, who in all the time he had been there, had not told the girl he was a king.

And so the farmer's daughter became a queen and lived happily ever after.

The Genie

Once, a lazy servant girl was polishing a silver jug when, to her surprise, a genie appeared.

"I will grant you three wishes," he said.

"I wish that this silver was clean," said the servant girl. She looked back down at the silver and saw that it was **gleaming** and clean.

The next day the servant girl was sewing clothes and decided to use her second wish.

"I wish that this sewing was finished," she said. She looked at the sewing and saw that it was done.

Fed up with hard work, the girl wished that she was no longer a servant. Her third wish came true at once. She was no longer a servant. The girl had become a beggar on the streets.

The girl began to cry at her terrible mistake. The genie took pity on her and appeared in a puff of smoke.

"In future, be **careful** what you wish for," said the genie. And he sent her back to her life as a servant. The girl did her work more happily from then on.

Eeny, Meeny

Eeny, meeny, miney, mo,
Catch a tiger by the toe,
If he squeals let him go,
Eeny, meeny, miney, mo.

Solomon Grundy

Solomon Grundy,
Born on a Monday,
Christened on Tuesday,
Married on Wednesday,
Took ill on Thursday,
Grew worse on Friday,
Died on Saturday,
Buried on Sunday.
That was the end of
Solomon Grundy.

Two Little Dickie Birds

Two little dickie birds sitting on a wall,
One named Peter, one named Paul.
Fly away Peter, fly away Paul,
Come back Peter, come back Paul!

Five Fat Peas

Five fat peas in a pea-pod pressed,
One grew, two grew, so did all the rest.
They grew, and grew, and did not stop,
Until one day,
The pod went POP!

One, Two, Three, Four, Five

One, two, three, four, five,
Once I caught a fish alive.
Six, seven, eight, nine, ten,
Then I let it go again.
Why did you let it go?
Because it bit my finger so.
Which finger did it bite?
This little finger on the right.

One Potato, Two Potato

One potato, two potato,
Three potato, four.
Five potato,
Six potato,
Seven potato,
MORE!

The Sun and the Wind

The sun and the wind were arguing one day.

"I am **stronger** than you," said the sun.

"What rubbish," said the wind. "I am far stronger than you."

"See that man down there?" the sun asked the wind, "I am so strong that I bet I could get that coat off him."

"You're not strong enough to do that," said the wind. "I could easily get that coat off him."

"Alright," said the sun. "You go first."

So the wind **blew** with all his might and strength. Leaves blew off the trees and tiles blew off the roof tops. But the man only pulled his coat more tightly around him. The wind could not get the coat off the man.

"Now it's my turn," said the sun. And he **shone** down on the man. The strength of the sun was so fierce that the man quickly became very hot. He became so hot that he took off his coat and slung it over his shoulder.

"I win!" said the sun.

"Oh, blow!" said the wind.

The Three Wishes

It was Princess Felicity's birthday and the royal magician had granted her three wishes.

She knew at once what her first wish would be.

"I wish I had long, golden hair," she said. Right away her hair started to grow... and grow... and grow. It wouldn't stop!

"I wish I had a pair of scissors," she said. And in the twinkling of an eye, a pair of scissors appeared. Princess Felicity cut her hair, but the more she cut it the more it grew.

Princess Felicity's hair was getting out of control. Soon the whole room would be filled with the golden hair. Something had to be done, quickly.

"I wish I had my old hair back again," she said. And in a flash she had her hair back as it always had been.

"I'll never moan about my hair again," said the little princess.

Princess Felicity still enjoyed her birthday. The royal wig-maker collected up all the golden hair that the princess had cut off, and used it to make a beautiful golden wig. Now Princess Felicity could have long, golden hair whenever she felt like a change – it hadn't been such a bad hair day after all!

The Princess
and the Fool

There was once a rich fool who had a very clever servant. The rich fool came to hear of a princess who wanted to marry a clever man. Thinking himself to be clever, he went to see her.

The princess decided to see how **clever** the rich fool was.

"If a cockerel laid an egg on top of a hill, which side of the hill would it roll down?" she asked.

The fool went away and, after a day of rolling eggs down a hill, he felt sure he knew the answer.

As the rich fool began to tell the princess, his servant began to **laugh.** He laughed so much he couldn't stop.

"What's so funny?" asked the puzzled fool.

"The egg wouldn't roll down either side of the hill. Cockerels do not lay eggs –
hens do!"

The princess decided
that the servant was
clever and also
very funny – so
she married him
instead! And they
lived a happy life
filled with laughter.

The Travelling Minstrel

One day, a travelling minstrel wandered into a kingdom, singing of some golden treasure that he was seeking.

"When I find the golden treasure, it will be for my own pleasure," sang the minstrel. One by one, people began to follow him.

"If he knows where gold is, I'm going too," said one woman. Soon the minstrel had a crowd of people behind him, all talking about how they would spend the treasure.

"I'm going to buy a new horse," said a farmer.

"I would like a new dress," said a woman.

After a long time, the minstrel sat down on a hillside. "What a lovely view," he said, looking down on a field of beautiful golden wheat.

The followers felt foolish when they realised that the beautiful view was the treasure that the minstrel had been singing about. But they had to admit, it was a lovely view!

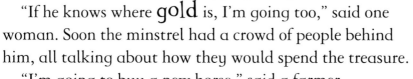

The Jumblies

They went to sea in a sieve, they did,
In a sieve they went to sea.
In spite of all their friends could say,
On a winter's morn, on a stormy day,
In a sieve they went to sea!
And when the sieve turned round and round,
And everyone cried, "You'll all be drowned!"
They called aloud, "Our sieve ain't big,
But we don't care a button! We don't care a fig!

The Jumblies

In a sieve we'll go to sea!"
Far and few, far and few,
Are the lands where the Jumblies live;
Their heads are green, and their hands are blue,
And they went to sea in a sieve.

And in twenty years they all came back,
In twenty years or more.
And everyone said, "How tall they've grown!
For they've been to the Lakes, and the Torrible Zone,
And the hills of the Chankly Bore!"
And they drank their health, and gave them a feast
Of dumplings made of beautiful yeast.
And everyone said, "If we only live,
We too will go to sea in a sieve,
To the hills of the Chankly Bore!"
Far and few, far and few,
Are the lands where the Jumblies live;
Their heads are green, and their hands are blue,
And they went to sea in a sieve.

The Princess Who Would Not Speak

There was once a princess who wouldn't speak. Her mother offered her **wonderful** treats to try and persuade her to talk, but still she wouldn't utter a word.

One day, the king offered a bag of gold coins to the person who could make his daughter speak. People lined up to try their luck, but nobody could make her talk.

An old peasant woman came to hear of the reward. She put a **chicken** on her head and set off to the palace, getting a few funny looks on the way.

When the old woman met the princess, she made small talk, but never once mentioned the chicken on her head. After some time, the hen gave a **squawk** and laid an egg which fell to the ground with a **splat!** The old woman continued to talk about this and that, as if nothing had happened.

The princess couldn't stop herself. "Did you know that you have a **chicken** on your head?" she asked. The king was delighted and paid the old woman a bag of gold. She and her chicken went home happy.

The Prince and the Peasant

Once there was a young prince who wanted to go exploring. By chance, he met a peasant boy who looked **exactly** like him. He realised that, if they swapped clothes, he would get his wish. The peasant boy agreed and, as soon as they swapped, the prince felt a hand on his shoulder. "There you are lad," said a **gruff** voice.

The prince was led away and put to work in a field. It was hard work and by the time he had finished he was very **hungry.** But all he got for his supper was a thin soup and a crust of bread.

The next day, the prince and the boy changed back into their own clothes. "When I am king, I promise to make sure that nobody goes hungry," he told the boy.

The prince grew up and, when he was king, he did not forget his promise.

The River

Moody river, running fast,
Deep and foaming as you pass.
Rain has swelled your water high,
Murky swirls go sweeping by.

Angry now, you froth and churn
The water reeds, which twist and turn.
The ducks all hide beneath their wings,
The wildlife shelters, no birds sing.

The River

Until the torrents heave a sigh,
And clouds are lifting from the sky.
Calm descends, the storm has gone.
The water's still, the sun is strong.

The peaceful river's clear at last.
The sparkling water ambles past
And finds its way quite happily,
Through green fields, then out to sea.

The riverbank's alive and green,
The gurgling water's fresh and clean.
The fish can jump, the ducklings float,
And I can row my rowing boat.

Pat-a-Cake, Pat-a-Cake

Pat-a-cake, pat-a-cake, baker's man,
Bake me a cake as fast as you can.
Pat it and prick it and mark it with B,
And put it in the oven for Baby and me!
For Baby and me, for Baby and me,
Put it in the oven for Baby and me.

I'm a Little Teapot

I'm a little teapot, short and stout,
Here's my handle, here's my spout.
When I get my steam up hear me shout,
Tip me up and pour me out.

Spin, Dame

Spin, Dame, spin
Your bread you must win;
Twist the thread and break it not,
Spin, Dame, spin.

Round and Round the Garden

Round and round the garden
Like a teddy bear;
One step, two steps,
Tickle you under there!

Ride a Cock-Horse

Ride a cock-horse to Banbury Cross
To see a fine lady upon a white horse.
With rings on her fingers and bells on her toes,
She shall have music wherever she goes.

To Market, To Market

To market, to market, to buy a fat pig,
Home again, home again, jiggety-jig.
To market, to market, to buy a fat hog,
Home again, home again, jiggety-jog.
To market, to market, to buy a plum cake,
Home again, home again, market is late.
To market, to market, to buy a plum bun,
Home again, home again, market is done.

The Princess and the Moon

There was once a princess who got everything she wanted right away. But one day, the princess asked her father for something **impossible**.

"Daddy, can I have the moon?" she asked.

Her father tried everything to bring down the moon, but nothing worked. "I'm afraid you can't have the moon because it is too **big** to bring down from the sky," the king told his daughter.

"But when I look at it, it's just a tiny silver ball no bigger than my thumbnail," replied the puzzled princess. So the king asked his silversmith to make a tiny silver moon, which he gave to his daughter.

"Thank you, Daddy, it's so beautiful," she said.

When the moon appeared in the sky that night, the king was worried she would realise her moon wasn't the **real** one. But the princess didn't mind.

"The moon has grown back again, of course," she said. "It's always growing and shrinking!'

The Lazy Prince

There was once a prince who was very lazy indeed. His mother put him to work in the stables to teach him a lesson.

One day a princess rode by and, thinking the prince was a stable boy, asked him to give some water to her horse.

"The water's right in front of you," said the lazy prince. "Why don't you do it yourself?"

"Do it **myself?**" said the princess, who was even lazier than the prince. "I really can't be bothered."

The prince liked the look of the princess. The two of them talked for a while and, when he could be bothered, he told the princess that he was actually a prince.

The lazy prince and princess got to know each quite well, and they eventually (it took them a while to get around to it) got married.

The Fortunate Prince

There was once a handsome prince called Alexander who
set off to seek his fortune. "When I return I will be older and
wiser," he told his family.

Wherever he went, people were kind to him. Ordinary
people made a special effort to feed and entertain him. The
prince thought that this was their usual everyday life.

One day, when the prince had been travelling for a few
weeks, he rode into a thick forest and realised that he was
lost. After a long time, Prince Alexander noticed the turrets of
a grand castle in the distance. "How fortunate," he thought.
"The people who live there will surely look after me."

The prince rode through the thick forest, which was
overgrown with brambles. When he finally reached the castle
there was nobody to be seen, but he heard a beautiful voice
singing a sad song. As if enchanted,
he followed the sound and
soon found himself in
a small room at
the top of a tower.
Sitting by the
window singing, was
the most **beautiful
girl** he had ever seen!

"What are you
doing here all alone?"

asked the prince. "And why are you singing such a sad song?"

"I am Princess Sophia," explained the mysterious girl. "I used to live here with my family and servants, but I was so ungrateful, spoilt and bossy that they left me here to look after myself."

The princess had learned to grow vegetables, cook and sew. She could look after herself but was very lonely.

The prince set off for home, taking Sophia with him. They rode back the way he had come, but his clothes had been torn by the brambles and he no longer looked like royalty. So the prince and princess were treated just like anyone else. Everybody was hard at work but they still shared their food, although they had little to spare.

When the prince returned home he was indeed a little older, but **much** wiser. He now knew things were different outside his castle gates and that he was fortunate to be a prince.

The prince and the princess were married in a beautiful ceremony, which they prepared themselves. Everyone was invited, including Princess Sophia's family – who were delighted to see that their daughter had changed for the better!

Ring-a-Ring o'Roses

Ring-a-ring o'roses,
A pocket full of posies.
Atishoo! Atishoo!
We all fall down.

Row, Row, Row your Boat

Row, row, row your boat,
Gently down the stream.
Merrily, merrily, merrily, merrily,
Life is but a dream.

Row, row, row your boat,
Gently down the stream.
If you see a crocodile,
Don't forget to **scream!**

The Man in the Moon

The man in the moon
Looked out of the moon,
Looked out of the moon and said,
"It's time for all children on the Earth
To think about getting to bed."

Three Young Rats

Three young rats with black felt hats,
Three young ducks with white straw flats,
Three young dogs with curling tails,
Three young cats with demi-veils,
Went out to walk with two young pigs
In satin vests and sorrel wigs,
But suddenly it chanced to rain
And so they all went home again.

Teddy Bear, Teddy Bear

Teddy bear, teddy bear,
Touch the ground.
Teddy bear, teddy bear,
Turn around.
Teddy bear, teddy bear,
Walk upstairs.
Teddy bear, teddy bear,
Say your prayers.
Teddy bear, teddy bear,
Turn out the light.
Teddy bear, teddy bear,
Say goodnight.

An Elephant Walks

An elephant walks like this and that;
He's terribly tall and he's terribly fat.
He's got no fingers,
He's got no toes,
But goodness gracious
What a long, long nose!

This Little Piggy

This little piggy went to market,
This little piggy stayed at home,
This little piggy had roast beef,
This little piggy had none,
And this little piggy cried,
"Wee, wee, wee, wee, wee!"
All the way home.

Incy Wincy Spider

Incy Wincy spider climbed up the spout,
Down came the rain and washed the spider out.
Out came the sun, and dried up all the rain,
Incy Wincy Spider climbed up the spout again.

The Magic Mirror

There was once a magic mirror that could show the future.

One day, a courtier to the prince looked in the magic mirror and was **horrified** to see the prince being robbed. He had seen the face of the robber quite clearly, so the courtier decided to be on the lookout for this scoundrel.

A few days later, the courtier was walking through a forest with the prince, when he saw the rogue in the mirror coming towards them.

"Look out, your majesty!" he shouted, as the man ran towards them.

The man from the mirror rushed at the prince, knocking him sideways. Just seconds later, a tree came crashing down, narrowly missing them all.

Everything the courtier had seen in the mirror had come true – but not in the way he had expected. The man he saw was not a robber after all. He was pushing the prince away from the falling tree. The so-called robber had saved the prince's life!

From then on, the courtier looked at things a lot more carefully, and stopped jumping to conclusions.

The Joker Prince

There was once a prince who was always playing tricks on people. Once, he balanced a bucket of water over the kitchen door and the bucket tipped over and soaked the chef. Everyone was fed up with the prince's practical jokes.

But one day, the prince met his match. There was a princess visiting the palace and the prince had placed a whoopee cushion on her chair at breakfast. The princess was very annoyed and vowed to pay him back.

The princess could throw her voice to sound as if it was coming from another direction. That afternoon, when the prince was playing with his dog, she hid and threw her voice to make it sound as if the dog was talking. "I suppose you think your tricks are funny," the dog appeared to say.

"W-w-what?" stuttered the prince. He couldn't believe his ears.

"Stop being such a pain," the voice went on. "Nobody likes your tricks."

The prince was so shocked that he stopped playing tricks on people. He spent many hours coaxing his dog to talk again, but he never succeeded!

A Prince in Disguise

There was once a prince who was very bored with his life, even though he could do anything he pleased. "I'm bored of being a prince, so I'll try being someone different for a change," he thought. And he **disguised** himself as a kitchen boy.

The disguised prince crept into the kitchen and mingled with his servants who were all very busy, rushing about.

"His Majesty wants his grapes peeled," said the butler, thrusting a silver platter piled high with grapes at the disguised prince. "Look lively and start on this lot, or we'll all be in **trouble** at lunchtime."

"And after that you can pick out all of the raisins from this cereal," chipped in the cook. "His Majesty finds them too chewy."

The disguised prince sat there peeling grapes, picking out raisins and even ironing his own socks. He realised how hard everybody worked to look after him.

By lunchtime, the prince was dressed as himself again. He felt **exhausted** and a little bit silly.

From that day on, the servants noticed a change in the prince. He stopped asking them to do silly things, and he did a lot more for himself. So much more, in fact, that he rarely had the time to feel bored!

The Old Beggar Woman

Once a carriage came into a village carrying a royal party. A beggar woman asked them for some food, but they refused her and drove off, **splashing** the old woman.

When the royal party next sat down to eat, everything tasted bitter. Soon everyone at the palace became very **hungry** indeed.

"This must be what that old beggar feels like every day," said the princess.

A few days later the royal coach passed through the village again. This time they stopped to give the beggar woman some food. When they next sat down to eat, they found that their food tasted absolutely **delicious.** They savoured every mouthful, and were never so selfish again.

The Rainbow's End

How did it get there, so pretty and bright?
It must be a magical fairy light.
Shimmering colours, up so high,
A beautiful rainbow, painting the sky!

Is it a wonderful fairyland slide,
Where pixies and fairies can go for a ride?
I'd like to follow it, because I'm told
At the **rainbow's end** is a pot of gold!

The Princess and the Donkey

There was once a very bossy princess who always got her own way, and if she didn't – she would **scream** until she did.

One day, she was walking in her rose garden when she found a donkey had strayed into it.

"Get out of my garden!" she shouted at the donkey. But the donkey did not budge. The princess started to scream, but the donkey just folded in his ears and stood firm. The princess was **furious** and tried everything to make the donkey leave her garden, but the donkey would not go.

By the time the donkey's owner came along, the princess was red in the face with anger. The donkey's owner gave his creature a gentle stroke on its head.

"Come on girl," said the donkey's cheerful owner, and the cheeky beast happily followed him out of the rose garden.

Laughing merrily, the owner called back over his shoulder, "You only had to ask nicely!"

The princess should have learned her lesson after this, but I'm afraid to say that she did not!

Goldilocks and the Three Bears

Once upon a time, Goldilocks was playing in the woods near her home. Her beautiful long, blonde curls tumbled down her back as she skipped along the path. Goldilocks stopped and sniffed the air… she could smell something **yummy!**

Feeling hungry, Goldilocks followed the trail and soon found herself in front of a little house.

"How sweet," she cried, clapping her hands in delight. "I wonder who lives here…"

Goldilocks knocked loudly on the front door. Nobody was at home but the door was unlocked, so Goldilocks went in. She saw a kitchen table with three bowls on it. "I'm sure no one will mind if I just have a little taste of this porridge," she told herself. Goldilocks picked up a spoon and started to eat from the biggest bowl of porridge.

"Yuck!" she cried, shaking her golden hair. "This porridge is far too salty!"

Goldilocks tried the medium-sized bowl.

"Yuck!" she gasped. "This porridge is far too sweet!"

There was still the small bowl to try. Goldilocks took a little mouthful. "Mmmm!" she sighed, licking her lips. "This porridge is perfect!" And she ate it all up.

Yawn! Goldilocks began to feel sleepy. In the living room, she saw three armchairs.

There was a big chair, a medium-sized chair and a tiny little chair.

Goldilocks climbed onto the biggest chair. "This chair is too big!" she sighed.

Next, Goldilocks clambered onto the medium-sized chair. "This chair is a bit too lumpy!" cried Goldilocks.

Then, Goldilocks tried the tiny chair. "This chair is perfect!" beamed Goldilocks happily. She wiggled and jiggled around to get even more comfy when… Cr-r-r-ack! The chair broke into little pieces.

"Oh, no!" Goldilocks gasped. "Maybe I'll find somewhere else to lie down instead." And so Goldilocks walked up the stairs as bold as brass.

Upstairs, Goldilocks found three beds. There was a big bed, a medium-sized bed and a tiny little bed.

Goldilocks jumped up and down on each bed.

The big bed was too hard, the medium-sized bed was too soft, and the little bed was… **"Perfect!"** Goldilocks sighed happily. And the little girl crawled under the covers and fell fast asleep.

Meanwhile, three hungry bears returned to the house in the wood. They had been for a walk while their hot porridge cooled down. But the door was wide open and there were muddy footprints inside. The bears followed the footprints into the kitchen, and saw at once that someone had been there.

"Who's been eating my porridge?" growled Daddy Bear.

"Who's been eating my porridge?" gasped Mummy Bear.

"Who's been eating my porridge," squeaked Baby Bear, "and eaten it all up?"

Feeling shocked and confused, the three bears padded into the living room and saw that someone had been there, too.

"Who's been sitting in my chair?" roared Daddy Bear.

"Who's been sitting in my chair?" growled Mummy Bear.

"Who's been sitting in my chair,'" yelped Baby Bear, "and broken it?"

Suddenly, the three bears heard snoring from upstairs.

Daddy Bear, Mummy Bear and Baby Bear rushed up the stairs and went into the bedroom.

"Who's been sleeping in my bed?" roared Daddy Bear.

"Who's been sleeping in my bed?" growled Mummy Bear.

"Who's been sleeping in my bed," squeaked Baby Bear, pointing to Goldilocks, "and is still there?"

Goldilocks woke up with a start and found three bears peering down at her.

She jumped out of bed, ran out of the house and through the woods as fast as she could.

And the three bears never saw Goldilocks again.

The Magic Well

There was once a magic well that could answer questions. One day, a girl asked it when she would marry. The well whispered to her: *"On a silver steed, a stranger will call. He will be your groom when the leaves start to fall."*

One autumn evening, as the sun was going down, a young man rode into town on a horse that glinted silver in the setting sun. The girl noticed him right away and thought it must be the stranger on the silver steed that the well had spoken of. She and the stranger fell in love. But the next day, the girl realised that the horse wasn't silver but white. The setting sun had only made the horse look silver. So the girl went back to the well.

"Will I marry this man?" she asked. And the well whispered: *"The silvery light of love is cast, upon your own true love at last."*

The well's prediction was right, and the girl married her true love in that same silvery light of the low autumn sun.

The Foolish Shepherd

A shepherd was singing one day, when he heard
someone singing back to him. He was very puzzled.

"Who's there?" he called.

"Who's there?" came the reply.

"My name's Paul," said the shepherd.

"My name's Paul," came the reply.

"I'm a shepherd," called the shepherd.

"I'm a shepherd," came the reply.

The shepherd was astonished. He
knew he was the only shepherd in those hills.

"If you're a shepherd, prove it," shouted the shepherd.

"If you're a shepherd, prove it," came the reply.

"I can make my sheep bleat," he cried, and then he chased
his sheep until they bleated, and stopped to listen.

"I can make my sheep bleat," came the reply, along with
lots of bleating. The shepherd was extremely baffled and didn't
know what to think. Who was this other shepherd?

As the shepherd herded his sheep back down the hill, he
thought it sounded as if the sheep were laughing at him –
perhaps, unlike the shepherd, they knew what an echo was!

The Enchanted Apple Tree

There was once an enchanted apple tree that only gave fruit once every ten years and, when it did, villagers came to pick the delicious apples and **make a wish**.

There was a little girl in the village called Pomona. She had heard all about the tree but had never tasted its delicious fruit, so when spring came that year and she saw the tree in blossom she was very excited and began to wonder what she might wish for.

When the apples were ready, Pomona picked one and took a bite. It was delicious! Her parents asked what she had wished for, and she told them that she could not think of anything she wanted. Her parents were happy to hear this. They explained to Pomona that their wish ten years ago was that they should have a daughter who would be so content that she should wish for nothing more than she had. Their wish had come true!

The Magic Cloak

There was once a woman who had a magic cloak. Whenever she wore it, people would believe every word she spoke, whether it was the truth or not. She used the magic cloak to make people do whatever she wanted them to.

She told one poor farmer that his grain was not worth more than a penny a sack, and so she bought her grain cheaply and the farmer grew poorer.

This wicked woman had a servant who found out about the magic cloak and was very annoyed with her for treating people this way. The servant, who was extremely clever, came up with a plan: she turned the magic cloak **inside out!** Her mistress put on the cloak and went off to cause some mischief. But when the woman spoke, she found she could only speak the **truth.**

When talking again to the farmer, she told him that his grain was the finest in the county and she should pay one hundred times more than she had.

As word of her behaviour went around the village, all those she had wronged came to see her and she could not help but tell them the truth. All her wrongs were put right. The woman was very puzzled and never wore the cloak again.

A Special Day at Fairy School

It was Woodland Day in Fairyland, a special day when the fairies use their magic especially to help the woodland creatures. All the pupils at Fairy School were very excited because this year they were allowed to join in by practising their helpful spells. Isabella and Chloe, the youngest fairies of all, had been looking forward to this day for weeks.

Now the big day had arrived and all the fairies were busy helping. Aiden used his **magic** to help a spider mend her broken web. Holly helped a bee to find some nectar to drink. Their teacher, Mrs Spritely, was very pleased.

But Isabella and Chloe were sad because they couldn't make their magic work. They had tried to help a caterpillar turn into a butterfly but nothing had happened.

"Good try," said Mrs Spritely.

Chloe and Isabella **sighed** so deeply as they flew past a tree, that two little birds popped their heads out of their nest.

"Tweet! Tweet! Why are you both so sad?"

"We wanted to practise our magic, but we can't find anyone who needs our help," said Isabella.

"You can help us!" chirped the happy little chicks. They explained that they hadn't learned to fly yet and that they wanted to leave their nest and join in with all the fun of Woodland Day. Isabella and Chloe waved their magic wands over the two birds who instantly began to rise from their nest.

"Now flap your wings," cried Chloe. The spell had worked! Isabella and Chloe flew around the treetops with their fluffy new friends.

"Excellent work!" said Mrs Spritely, as Isabella and Chloe glowed with pride. They both decided that this had been the best Woodland Day ever!

The Perfect Snowflake

One morning, Emma woke up to find something magical happening outside her bedroom window.

"It's snowing!" she whispered excitedly, her warm breath making misty patterns on the glass.

Outside, snowflakes swirled and twirled in the air before floating to the ground.

Emma had never seen anything so beautiful.

"If only I could have a snowflake of my own to keep!" she thought.

In the garden, Emma caught lots of snowflakes, but each one disappeared when she tried to show her mum.

"Snowflakes melt when they're warm," Mummy explained.

"But I wanted to keep one!" Emma sighed.

Later that day, the sun shone just as the last few snowflakes fell.

They **shimmered** in the light like sparkly diamonds, before vanishing onto the ground.

That afternoon, Mummy showed Emma how to make a paper snowflake.

"It's not the same as having a real snowflake," Emma sighed. She remembered what it was like to play in the snow:

Real snowflakes dance in the sky.

Real snowflakes sparkle in the sun.

Real snowflakes dazzle like diamonds in the snow!

Emma couldn't wait to play with **real** snowflakes again.

But the next morning, when Emma went outside to play, all the snow had melted. Just then, the most perfect snowflake Emma had ever seen fluttered in the sky.

This snowflake danced in the sky... sparkled in the sun, and... **dazzled like a diamond.**

But this snowflake wasn't real. It was made of paper, with sparkly sequins and glitter sprinkled on top. Emma hugged Mummy. "This snowflake is definitely one I can keep," she grinned.

Ballerina Bella and the Lucky Locket

Bella was looking forward to her ballet class after school.

"I hope you'll pay attention," Mum told her. She knew that Bella sometimes found it hard to concentrate.

"Of course I will," said Bella.

But it wasn't quite that easy. Each ballet lesson was the same. Just when Bella most needed to pay attention, something interesting would happen and she would get distracted.

At her ballet class that day, her teacher, Miss Ross, told the class that they were to put on a show. Everyone was very excited.

"You really must **pay attention** now, Bella," said Miss Ross. "You'll be dancing in front of an audience soon."

But when the girls started dancing, Bella noticed that Miss Ross wasn't concentrating very hard herself. She kept glancing around the room, as if she was looking for something.

As Bella and her friends began their rehearsal, Bella saw something interesting poking out from underneath the curtain.

The other girls started to dance back across the stage, but Bella disappeared off the stage.

"Bella!" called Miss Ross. "This really is too much!"

"What's this?" asked Bella, running onto the stage with something shiny in her hands.

"You've found it!" smiled the teacher, taking a necklace from Bella and holding it up for all the class to see.

"This is the prize my ballet teacher gave to me when I was best dancer in my first show. It's a lucky locket. I wanted to give it to the best dancer in our show, but I thought I had lost it. Thank you, Bella. Where did you find it?"

But Bella didn't answer. Her eyes were closed. She saw herself on stage, wearing the locket. She saw herself dancing better than she had ever danced in her life.

Bella kept this picture in her head. When she began to dance at the show, she **imagined** herself dancing without making a single mistake. But it wasn't a dream.

On the night of the show, Bella did dance perfectly. And when she stepped to the front of the stage to take her bow as the best ballerina, the lucky locket was **sparkling** around her neck.

Little Jack Jingle

Little Jack Jingle,
He used to live single:
But when he got tired of this kind of life,
He left off being single, and lived with his wife.

Harry Parry

O rare Harry Parry,
When will you marry?
When apples and pears are ripe.
I'll come to your wedding,
Without any bidding,
And dance and sing all the night.

Little Tommy Tittlemouse

Little Tommy Tittlemouse,
Lived in a little house;
He caught fishes
In other men's ditches.

Young Roger Came Tapping

Young Roger came tapping at Dolly's window,
Thumpaty, thumpaty, thump!
He asked for admittance, she answered him "No!"
Frumpaty, frumpaty, frump!
"No, no, Roger, no! As you came you can go!"
Stumpaty, stumpaty, stump!

Jack, Jack, the Bread's A-Burning

Jack, Jack, the bread's a-burning,
All to a cinder;
If you don't come and fetch it out
We'll throw you through the window.

Little Jumping Joan

Here am I, little jumping Joan.
When nobody's with me,
I'm always alone.

Little Red Riding Hood

Once there was a little girl who always wore a red cape and hood. Everyone called her Little Red Riding Hood.

"Your granny isn't feeling well today," said Little Red Riding Hood's mother one morning. "Take this basket of food to her, but stay on the path and don't talk to any strangers on the way."

So Little Red Riding Hood skipped off into the woods to visit her granny. On the way, she noticed some pretty blue flowers growing just a little way off the path. "I'll just pick a few for Granny and then I'll be on my way," she thought.

But Little Red Riding Hood was not alone.

"Hello, little girl," said a deep growling voice. Little Red Riding Hood looked up and saw a wolf.

"Where are you off to?" asked the wolf.

"I'm going to visit my granny," replied Little Red Riding Hood,

who had already forgotten her mother's warning.

As Little Red Riding Hood continued along the path, the wolf ran as fast as he could to her granny's house. When he got there, he ate the granny in one big gulp! Then he disguised himself as the granny, climbed into bed and waited.

Soon, Little Red Riding Hood arrived.

"Granny, what big eyes you have," she said.

"All the better to see you with," replied the wolf.

"What big ears you have," went on the little girl.

"All the better to hear you with," replied the wicked wolf.

"And what big teeth you have," she said.

"All the better to eat you with!" said the wolf, and he swallowed her in one gulp! Then the wolf fell soundly asleep.

Luckily, a woodcutter was passing the cottage and heard the wolf's loud snores. He went into the cottage, grabbed the wolf and turned him upside down. Then he shook him and shook him until... out fell Little Red Riding Hood and her granny! The woodcutter, Little Red Riding Hood and her granny chased the wolf away. And he was never seen again.

King Canute and the Sea

King Canute was a powerful king. His courtiers were always **flattering** him so that they could stay in his favour.

One day, the king's courtiers persuaded him that he was so powerful that he would be able to **stop** the tide coming in.

King Canute, believing their flattery, went down to the beach and sat on his throne waiting for the tide to turn so that he could command it to stop.

"I command you to stop," he bellowed as the sea came in. But the tide did not stop. King Canute sat steadfast on his throne. "I command you to stop," he bellowed again, but still the sea paid no heed.

The courtiers backed away as the sea came closer, but still the king would not leave his throne. When the sea began to cover the king's feet, he realised that he was not as powerful as he'd thought. He ruled more wisely from then on.

The Vain Princess and her Servant

There was once a very vain princess who was always looking in the mirror. Her servant, however, was far prettier, although she didn't even own a mirror. The servant found pleasure in the nature around her, and her **happiness** made her very pretty.

The princess was to be married, and many princes came to meet her. At first, she was very excited. But none of the princes asked for her hand in marriage. The vain princess was so upset that she ran out into the garden where she heard a beautiful melody. She saw that it was her servant **singing** happily. The servant held an armful of wild flowers and her eyes shone brightly. She looked so pretty!

The princess joined her servant and soon forgot her cares. She began to enjoy what she saw around her, and she stopped looking in the mirror. As the princess grew happier, she became **prettier.** News of her beauty spread far and wide. Princes lined up to ask for her hand, but she was too busy enjoying the wonders of the world to think about marriage, and so they had to wait.

The Prince and the Unicorn

Long ago, there lived a prince who knew the whereabouts of the only **unicorn** left in the world. Because unicorns' horns are magical, there were many evil people who wanted to kill the unicorn and get that magic. For this reason, the prince had vowed to the unicorn never to reveal his hiding place.

One day, the old king passed away and the prince became king and took a wife. The new queen was a beautiful woman, but not a kind one. One night, she heard the new king talking in his sleep. He said:

"Unicorn, unicorn, never shall I tell,
That across the lake is where you dwell.
In a hidden cave beyond the dell,
There you shall stay, hidden so well."

The next day the queen sent her huntsman out with instructions to find the poor unicorn and bring back his **magical** horn. The unicorn heard a human approaching and did not recognise his friend's familiar step, so he fled deep into the caves, and the very last unicorn was never seen again.

Perhaps he's there still.

The Stubborn Prince

Once there was a stubborn prince who would **never** do as he was told. His parents despaired of him for, one day, this stubborn boy would be king.

One windy day, a new governess arrived to teach the young prince. She arrived so suddenly it was as if the wind had blown her there. The governess looked ordinary, but there was more to her than met the eye. Lessons began right away, but the prince just folded his arms and pursed his lips.

The governess wasn't worried, "I know how to deal with stubborn boys," she thought. There was a **shimmer** of magical lights and a huge gust of wind blew in, lifted the prince up into the air and left him hovering beneath the ceiling. At first the prince was scared, but then he began to enjoy himself.

"**Ha, ha!** This is fun!" he laughed. "Do it again!" he called, as the chair began to sink down.

"Not until you've done your work," replied the governess. So the prince started to work, and every time he got something right, up he'd fly again. He soon found out that joining in was fun, and he was never stubborn again.

The Amethyst Brooch

Of all the treasures in the world, Ella liked her grandmother's amethyst brooch the best. It was a beautiful purple colour and glinted in the light when she held it up to the window. Every time she went to visit her granny, she would ask to see the special brooch, and was sometimes even allowed to wear it for a little while, which was the best treat ever.

"Tell me how you got the brooch," Ella asked one day when she was visiting. "Did Grandpa give it to you?"

Ella's granny beckoned her over to where she was sitting and Ella knew that she was about to hear a story.

"A very long time ago," began Ella's grandmother, "when I was just a young girl, I worked in a big house for a family. I cleaned the house for them and looked after the young children. I grew very fond of the family and they grew fond of me, and so I stayed there for many years. The lady of the house had a beautiful purple brooch and I used to admire it when I helped her dress for a party.

"One day, a chauffeur came to the house to drive a shiny new car for the family. He was so handsome in his uniform that I fell in love with him straight away. That man was your grandfather. Luckily he felt the same way and he asked me to marry him.

"On the evening before my wedding day, I was putting on my shawl ready to leave when I noticed something glinting – it was the beautiful **amethyst brooch!** The lady I worked for had pinned it onto my shawl as a surprise, because she knew how much I liked it. And I have treasured it ever since."

Brrrring! The doorbell rang and broke the spell of the story. Ella ran to answer the door. She knew it would be her mother because today was Ella's birthday and they were going home to have a birthday party. She ran to kiss her granny goodbye and thought she noticed a special **gleam** in her eyes.

As Ella put her coat on ready to leave, she noticed a **glint** of something purple on the collar, and realised that it was her grandmother's amethyst brooch!

"Happy birthday, Ella!" called her granny. "The brooch is yours now."

"Thank you, Granny!" said Ella. "I will treasure it **forever!"**

And she did.

The Timid Dragon

There was once a village that lived in fear of a dragon.

One day, a little girl called Rosa went out looking for wild flowers. She strayed off the path and found the **prettiest** flowers she had ever seen. As she began to pick them, she lost her footing and slid a little way down the mountain, twisting her ankle. She couldn't get up again, and so she began to cry.

She looked up and was terrified to see a fiery dragon's snout peeping out from behind a rock. Rosa **screamed,** the snout disappeared and Rosa began to cry louder. After a little while, she heard a soft gravelly sound and realised that it was the dragon singing. His song was so soothing that she felt less afraid. Soon the dragon peeped out again.

"Is it safe to come out now?" he asked.

"You won't eat me, will you?" asked Rosa.

"I was **worried** that you might hurt me," whispered the timid dragon. "Climb on my back and I'll fly you home."

When they arrived home, the villagers were scared, but Rosa told the dragon to sing his soothing song again. Soon everyone realised they had nothing to fear from him.

The villagers and the dragon lived together happily ever after.

The Princess Twins

Once upon a time, there were two pretty princess twins named Violet and Rose. They were identical. They each wore a ribbon in their hair; one **violet** and one **pink,** so that everyone knew which princess was which.

One day the princesses were feeling mischievous and decided to play a **trick** on their mother. Rosa put a violet ribbon in her hair so that now both twins looked like Violet. The two cheeky princesses put an empty picture frame in the garden.

"Mother," called Violet, "come and see our new mirror!"

The queen came out into the garden and saw Violet dancing in front of the mirror, and her reflection dancing back.

"What a **wonderful** mirror!" exclaimed the queen, as she went to see her own reflection.

But when she looked into the mirror, she was amazed to find she had no reflection.

The queen was puzzled... until she heard Rosa **giggling** from her hiding place behind a tree. Rosa, wearing her violet ribbon, had copied all of Violet's movements, and the queen had been fooled into believing that the empty frame was a mirror!

The Princess with Very Long Hair

A princess with very long hair,
Sat next to her window and stared
At the garden beyond
And a nice lily pond.
As she sat, she began to despair:

"Because of my very long hair,
To go for a walk, I don't dare.
I'd be bound to **fall** over
And land in the clover,
It's really **not** terribly fair!"

And so the royal barber was called
Snip! Snip! Now she's utterly **bald!**
But she has lots of fun,
Going out for a run;
Her mother, of course, is **appalled!**

The Fairy Queen's Lost Wand

One cold snowy day, Emma was playing in her garden. It had been a long winter, and she longed for spring.

Just then, Emma heard the sound of someone crying. "Who's there?" she called.

"It's me," sobbed a tiny voice. "Look behind the old tree stump and you'll see."

"I'm in terrible trouble," sobbed a tiny fairy, who was sitting on a pebble. "I've lost the queen's wand, and without it she can't start spring."

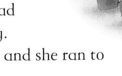

So that's why the winter had gone on so long. Suddenly, Ella remembered a stick she had found poking out of the snow. She had thought it interesting because it had shimmered in an unusual way.

"Wait there," she told the fairy, and she ran to fetch it.

The fairy was so happy to see the wand again and twinkled merrily before she vanished in a little puff of smoke.

The next morning, when Emma looked out of her window, she saw that the snow was melting and that little buds were growing on the trees. Spring was on its way at last!

Beauty and the Beast

Once, a girl called Beauty lived with her father and sisters.

One day her father was going to town and he asked his daughters what they would like him to bring them.

"I want a new dress," said the first sister.

"I want a new hat," said the second sister.

"I would like a **red rose,**" said Beauty.

The father bought the dress and hat, but he couldn't find a red rose anywhere.

On the way back, he passed a beautiful garden where he could see a red rose growing, so he picked one.

Suddenly, there was a terrible roar and an ugly beast appeared. **"Why have you stolen my rose?"** he said.

"It's for my daughter."

"Take the rose," said the Beast. "But give me your daughter in return, or you will die."

The father went home and told his daughters about the ugly Beast.

"I will go to the Beast," said Beauty, bravely.

The Beast's castle was warm and there was good food to eat, so

Beauty was comfortable there, although she missed her family. Every evening the ugly Beast appeared. He was **kind** to Beauty, so she grew to like him very much.

One evening, the Beast gave Beauty a magic mirror. When she looked into it, she saw that her father was sick.

"I must go to my father," said Beauty.

"Promise you will come back to me," said the Beast.

Beauty went home to look after her father. He was soon better, but she **forgot** her promise to the Beast.

One day, Beauty looked in the magic mirror and saw that the Beast was sick. Then she remembered her promise.

"I must go back to the Beast," said Beauty, and she hurried back to the castle. The Beast lay beside the red rose bush.

"Please do not die, Beast," said Beauty. **"I love you."**

As if by magic, the Beast changed into a handsome prince.

"I was under a **magic** spell," said the prince. "But your loving words, spoken from the heart, broke the spell."

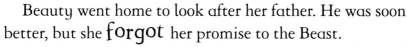

Soon after, Beauty and the prince were married, and they lived happily ever after.

Hot Cross Buns!

Hot cross buns!
Hot cross buns!
One a penny, two a penny,
Hot cross buns!
If you have no daughters,
Give them to your sons.
One a penny, two a penny,
Hot cross buns!

Catch It if You Can

Mix a pancake, beat a pancake,
Put it in a pan.
Cook a pancake, toss a pancake,
Catch it if you can!

Simple Simon

Simple Simon met a pieman going to the fair;
Said Simple Simon to the pieman,
"Let me taste your ware."
Said the pieman to Simple Simon,
"Show me first your penny."
Said Simple Simon to the pieman,
"Sir, I have not any!"

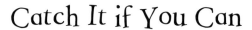

Georgie Porgie

Georgie Porgie, pudding and pie,
Kissed the girls, and made them cry.
When the boys came out to play,
Georgie Porgie ran away.

Willie Wastle

I Willie Wastle,
Stand on my castle,
And all the dogs of your town,
Will not drive Willie Wastle down.

Jack Sprat

Jack Sprat could eat no fat,
His wife could eat no lean;
And so, between the two of them,
They licked the platter clean.

Sleeping Beauty

Once upon a time, a king and queen had a beautiful baby girl.

"Let's have a party to celebrate," the king beamed.

"Oh, yes!" agreed the queen. "You send out the invitations, my dear. I am just so busy looking after the baby!"

The day of the party arrived. Tables were laden with delicious food and there was music and dancing in the great hall. One by one, the guests placed their presents beside the princess's cradle. Last of all, the four good fairies presented their gifts in a shower of fairy dust.

"You will be incredibly clever," said Whim.

"You will be a wonderful dancer," said Whirl.

"You will be a fabulous singer," said Whiny.

But before Wisp, the fourth good fairy could speak, there was a flash of lightning, followed by a wicked cackle. Ha! Ha! Ha!

A hush fell over the great hall. It was Wheedle, the wicked fairy. The king had forgotten to send her an invitation – and she was furious!

"Here's my gift," she shrieked. "One day, the princess will prick her finger on a spindle and die." Then she disappeared in a puff of black smoke.

Everyone gasped. The queen sobbed and the king shouted for the guards to burn every spinning wheel and spindle in the land.

Then Wisp fluttered up. "I cannot break the spell," she said, "but I can change it. If the princess does prick her finger, she will not die. She will fall into a deep sleep and will one day be woken by a kiss of true love."

The years passed and the princess grew up to be everything the good fairies had promised. Then one day, she was exploring the castle when she came across a secret door. It led to a tower she had never seen before. She climbed the steep staircase and entered a tiny room. There, in the corner, was a long-forgotten spinning wheel. The princess had never seen anything like it. She brushed off the cobwebs and pricked her finger. Instantly, she fell into a deep sleep, along with everyone else in the castle.

A hundred years rolled by and a giant hedge of thorns grew up around the castle. Many tried to cut their way through the thorns, but all failed. Then one day, a handsome prince came riding by. When he saw the tower poking up from the forest of

thorns, he became very curious.

He drew out his sword to hack his way through but somehow a path **magically** appeared before him.

At last the prince came to the castle. He walked past the snoring guards at the gate and stopped to admire the smart horses dozing in the stables. He almost tripped over the cook slumped beside her cooking pot. He bowed before the king and queen sleeping on their thrones. Then, as if in a trance, he was drawn up the steps of the tower.

As soon as the prince set eyes upon the princess, his heart leapt. He had never seen anyone so lovely in his life. He bent down and kissed her gently on the lips.

The princess opened her eyes and smiled. "I've had such a lovely sleep," she sighed.

As she spoke the words, everyone in the castle woke up and went about their tasks as if nothing had happened. The guards stood to attention, the grooms continued brushing the horses and the cook stirred her cooking pot.

The king and the queen were delighted. Not only had the handsome prince broken the wicked spell, but he was in love with their beautiful daughter.

"Excellent!" bellowed the king. "Let's have a royal wedding!"

The prince and princess were soon married and the king threw a fabulous party. He invited everyone, apart from the wicked fairy. Luckily, this time the good fairies cast a spell to make sure she stayed away and everything ran smoothly.

After the wedding, the prince and princess rode off on the prince's fine horse and lived happily ever after.

Rumpelstiltskin

Once upon a time, there was a miller who had a daughter.

One day the king rode by. "My daughter can spin straw into gold," said the miller, who was **nervous** and told the king the first silly thing that came into his head.

But the king believed the foolish man and took his daughter away. He locked her in a room full of straw.

"Spin this straw into **gold**," said the king. But the miller's daughter could not spin straw into gold and began to cry.

After crying for some time, a strange little man appeared.

"I know how to spin straw into gold," he said. "What will you give me if I help you?"

"I will give you my necklace," said the miller's daughter.

The little man spun all the straw into gold and then left.

When the king saw the piles of gold, he was very pleased.

He then took the miller's daughter to an even **bigger** room, full of straw. "If you can spin this straw into gold, I will marry you," said the king.

Again the girl began to cry and the little man came back to see her.

"I need your help, but I have nothing to give you," she sobbed.

"I will help you again," said the little man, "but in return you must give me your first **baby**." The girl reluctantly agreed.

The straw was spun into huge piles of gold and the little man left.

The king kept his **promise** and married the miller's daughter and before long, a baby was born. But when the little man came to take the baby, the queen began to cry as if her heart would break.

"I will not take your baby if you can **guess** my name," said the man. "I will give you until the morning to guess it."

That night, the queen went for a walk in the woods and, by chance, saw the little man dancing round a fire singing,

"My name is Rumpelstiltskin. Rumpelstiltskin is my name."

In the morning, the little man came to see the queen.

"Is your name Don or Ron?" asked the queen.

"No! No!" said the little man.

"Is it Bill?" asked the queen.

"No! No!" said the man. Then the queen said, "Is your name Rumpelstiltskin?"

"Yes! Yes!" said the little man, and off he ran away, never to be seen again.

The Tomboy Princess

Princess Lily didn't like wearing dresses.

"Trousers are better," she insisted. "How am I supposed to climb trees in a big **puffy** dress?"

"Princesses are not supposed to climb trees," complained her parents.

But that didn't stop Lily. She loved playing outdoors and was always getting into the kind of scrapes that weren't expected of a princess.

"Young lady," warned her father one day, "it's about time you started acting less like a stable boy and more like a princess."

The king decided that he would throw a fancy ball for his daughter, and then she would **have** to wear a dress and be lady-like.

On the day of the ball, Princess Lily was fed up. It was a sunny day and she wanted to be outside riding her horse and looking for adventure, not cooped up indoors getting ready for a silly ball.

The royal hairdresser was called to do Lily's hair.

"Tut! Tut!" he mumbled as he tried to fashion Lily's scruffy locks into something more sophisticated.

When the queen arrived with a big puffy pink dress, Princess Lily had no choice but to put it on.

"I look so silly," she complained. "It's just not me!"

But the queen told her that she looked just perfect, and as she walked into the ballroom there was a hush as all the guests admired her – she looked so lovely!

Waiting to greet her was a handsome young prince.

"May I have the honour of this dance?" asked the prince.

"I suppose so," replied Princess Lily, rather rudely.

As they danced, the princess couldn't help sighing and the prince asked her what the matter was. When the princess explained that she would rather be outside in the fresh air, the young prince was delighted.

"I find these balls rather dull, too," he confessed. The prince and princess waited until nobody was looking and sneaked away into the garden. They climbed trees, ran in the fresh air and had a wonderful time.

"This is the best ball ever," said the prince happily, "but I wouldn't want to be in your shoes when your mother sees the state of your dress!"

The Sprite of Spring

Light of foot and soft of wing,
In gently floats the Sprite of Spring.
She **flitters** here and **flutters** there –
Her fairy touch is everywhere.

See the yellow daffodils,
Spread across the fresh green fields?
The Sprite of Spring made them appear;
Their yellow blooms means she is near.

The blossom on the apple trees
Attracts the **buzzing** honey bees.
The trees have leaves, the birds all sing,
All thanks to the Sprite of Spring.

The Tree with the Golden Leaf

There was once a farmer who set off to cut down an old chestnut tree that no longer bore fruit. He was about to begin when he noticed that the tree had one **glistening** golden leaf. Thinking he was dreaming, he went to a nearby brook and splashed his face to wake himself up.

To his amazement, the brook spoke:

"Wash out your eyes and look again upon the chestnut tree. Although it bears no fruit, behold its 'treasures a-plenty."

The farmer took another careful look at the old tree and noticed baby birds, squirrels and insects. There were so many things in the tree that he hadn't noticed at first, but the golden leaf he had seen was gone.

The farmer picked up his axe and set off home. As he walked back along the brook, he thought he heard it talk to him again:

"All that glitters is not gold."

The Foolish Emperor

There was once an emperor who had more gold than he had sense. His subjects, however, worked hard and were very poor. Any spare money they had went in taxes to the emperor.

One day, a terrible illness spread through the land and crops lay rotting in the fields as the workers were too ill to harvest them.

The emperor was very annoyed because there was no wheat to make his bread and no oats for his porridge.

"The farmers are so selfish," he said, and he gave orders to have them all arrested. His soldiers were sent to gather up the farmers to put them in jail. Soon all the prisons were full.

The emperor went to his dungeons to make the farmers go back to work, but when he saw how unwell they were, he realised his own foolishness.

"I have been blind," said the emperor. He sent all his soldiers to bring in the harvest and ordered his servants to care for the farmers. Soon the harvest was in and the farmers were well enough to work again.

From then on, the emperor made wiser choices. His people paid fewer taxes and never went hungry again.

The Wise Old Pig

There was once a princess who had a wise old pig who would help to solve her problems. When the princess got married, she wanted to keep the pig, but her husband, the king, refused. So the princess built her pig a little house in the forest. At first she would visit it often, but soon she forgot all about her pig.

One day, the king was **wounded** and the wisest men in the kingdom couldn't heal him. It seemed nobody could help.

That night, the queen had a **strange dream** about a little house in the forest and, when she awoke, remembered her wise old friend. She set off at once to find the pig's little house.

"Dear old pig," said the queen, "I am sorry that I forgot you, but now I need your help." The pig walked back through the forest with the queen, and pointed out wild herbs with her wise old **snout.**

The queen made a poultice with the herbs and the king's wounds soon healed.

The king was so grateful to the pig that he allowed her to live in the palace. And there she stayed for the rest of her days, happily solving problems.

Little Jack Horner

Little Jack Horner sat in the corner,
Eating his Christmas pie;
He put in his thumb, and pulled out a plum,
And said, "What a good boy am I!"

Little Tommy Tucker

Little Tommy Tucker sings for his supper,
What shall we give him? Brown bread and butter.
How shall he cut it without a knife?
How shall he marry without a wife?

Peter, Peter

Peter, Peter, pumpkin eater,
Had a wife and couldn't keep her.
He put her in a pumpkin shell
And there he kept her, very well.

Pease Pudding Hot

Pease pudding hot, pease pudding cold,
Pease pudding in the pot, nine days old.
Some like it hot, some like it cold,
Some like it in the pot, nine days old.

Pop Goes the Weasel

Half a pound of tuppenny rice,
Half a pound of treacle.
That's the way the money goes,
Pop goes the weasel!
Up and down the city road,
In and out of the Eagle,
That's the way the money goes,
Pop goes the weasel!

Oats and Beans and Barley Grow

Oats and beans and barley grow,
Oats and beans and barley grow.
Do you or I or anyone know
How oats and beans and barley grow?

First the farmer sows his seed,
Then he stands and takes his ease.
He stamps his feet and claps his hands
And turns around to view the lands.

Cinderella

Once upon a time, there was a pretty young girl who lived with her father, stepmother and two stepsisters. The stepmother was unkind, and the stepsisters were mean.

Every day, the girl got up at dawn to cook and clean and wash and sew for her stepmother and stepsisters. Every night, the stepmother told the girl to sleep beside the fire. Soon the girl's clothes and hair were so grey with ash and cinders that everyone called her Cinderella.

One morning, a special invitation arrived. All the young women in the kingdom were invited to a ball at the royal palace so that the young prince could choose a bride.

The two stepsisters were very excited and ordered Cinderella around as she helped them get ready for the ball.

Cinderella **sighed.** She wished she could go with them. As an elegant carriage took her stepsisters to the ball, Cinderella sat beside the hearth and wept.

"I wish I could go to the ball," she cried.

Suddenly, a strange light filled the room. Cinderella looked up. A silvery glow surrounded a kind-looking woman with a glittering wand.

"Who are you?" asked Cinderella, blinking in wonder.

"I am your **fairy godmother,**" she said. "I've come to help you go to the ball."

"But how?" asked Cinderella.

"Find me a big pumpkin, a white mouse and a rat," replied the fairy godmother.

Cinderella found everything as quickly as she could. The fairy godmother waved her wand. The pumpkin changed into a **magnificent** golden coach, the white mouse became a white horse and the rat became a coachman.

With one last gentle tap of the wand, Cinderella's dusty dress became a shimmering ball gown. On her feet were two **sparkling** glass slippers.

"Now," said the fairy godmother, "you are ready for the ball. But at the stroke of midnight the magic will end, and everything will return to what it was."

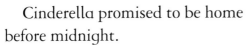

Cinderella promised to be home before midnight.

When Cinderella arrived at the palace, everyone turned to look at her. No one knew who Cinderella was, not even her own stepsisters.

The prince thought that she was the loveliest, most enchanting girl he had ever seen. He danced only with her.

As Cinderella whirled round the room in his arms, she felt so happy that she forgot her fairy godmother's warning.

Suddenly, she heard the clock chime… once, twice… twelve times!

"I must go!" cried Cinderella. And before the prince could stop her, she ran from the ballroom and out of the palace.

"Wait!" cried the prince, dashing after her. But by the time he reached the palace steps, she was gone.

Then he saw something twinkling on the steps – a single glass slipper. The prince picked it up.

"I will marry the woman whose foot fits this glass slipper," he declared. "I will search the kingdom until I find her."

The next day, the prince began going from house to house, looking for his true love. Every young woman in the kingdom tried on the glass slipper, but it didn't fit anyone.

At last, the prince came to Cinderella's house. Her stepsisters were waiting to try on the slipper.

The first stepsister pushed and squeezed, but she could barely get her fat toes into the tiny slipper.

The second stepsister also tried to cram her foot into the shoe. But it was no use.

The prince was turning to leave when a soft voice asked, "May I try the slipper, please?"

As Cinderella stepped forward to try on the slipper, her stepsisters began to laugh.

"Everyone should have a chance," said the prince, as he held out the sparkling slipper. And suddenly...

"Oh!" gasped her stepsisters.

Cinderella's dainty foot fitted into the slipper perfectly. As her stepsisters gazed in amazement, the prince joyfully took Cinderella in his arms.

Her stepsisters and stepmother were still trembling with shock as they watched Cinderella ride off in the prince's own carriage.

Cinderella and the prince were soon married, and lived happily ever after.

Let it Snow!

Olivia longed for snow. One morning when she woke up and looked out of her window, there it was – a **beautiful** blanket of snow covering her garden! She raced downstairs and ate her breakfast as quickly as possible. Olivia had plans that wouldn't wait. This year she was going to build the **best snowman ever!** Last year her neighbour, Jacob, had built a fantastic snowman. Everybody had admired it and the local newspaper had included a picture of it in a 'Winter Wonderland' snow feature. This year Olivia wanted *her* snowman to be the talk of the town.

Olivia set to work. She made a big snowball and rolled it through the snow watching it grow bigger and bigger, just as she had seen Jacob do the year before. Jacob was the best person she knew at **snowman** building, and she tried to remember exactly what he had done the year before. She was rolling another ball of snow for the head, when she realised something was missing. Where was Jacob? Surely he should be out by now, building his own snowman.

Olivia looked towards her neighbour's house and was surprised to see Jacob indoors and staring at her from behind the window.

She went over to his front door and instantly saw the problem – Jacob had a **broken arm!**

"I slipped on some ice last night," Jacob explained sadly. "The doctor said I need to rest my arm and keep it dry. Now I won't be able to build a snowman."

Olivia thought for a while and then smiled. "Wrap up warm and come outside," she told Jacob mysteriously.

Jacob sat grandly on the garden chair that Olivia had arranged for him, with his broken arm resting in a sling. Jacob gave Olivia instructions and she built the snowman just as he advised. The two friends made a great team, they just knew they'd make this year's 'Winter Wonderland' snow feature.

The next morning, Olivia rushed downstairs to see the local newspaper. Sure enough, there was her and Jacob's fantastic snowman. As she rushed out to show Jacob, she realised that the snow was melting and their snowman was almost gone.

"Never mind," Jacob told her. "We can build another snowman together next time it snows."

"And we'll always have this fantastic newspaper picture to remind us of this one!" added Olivia.

The Wicked Queen

Once there lived a very wicked queen, whose husband the king was as **good** as she was wicked. But everyone said that the king was just a bit too good. In fact, he could only see good in people, and seemed blind to the evil deeds of his wicked wife.

One day, when the queen was in a **particularly** bad mood, she locked one of the servants in a cupboard. When the servant complained of this bad treatment to the king, he just said that it must have been a mistake.

"My lovely wife would never do such a dreadful thing," he told the servant.

The next day, a young maid was cleaning the queen's room. She was late finishing and knew she would be punished if the queen found her still there. So, when the poor young maid heard the queen approaching, she hid under the bed.

The maid peeped out and saw the queen enter the room. She was astonished to see the queen open up a golden box and take from it a **crystal** bottle. The queen opened the bottle and carefully poured three drops of liquid from it into a silver goblet.

"**Ha, ha!**" laughed the queen. "When the king drinks my magic potion, he sees only good things, and never sees the **misery** I create."

The maid could hardly believe her own eyes and knew that there was only one thing to do. She crept over to the golden box, opened the crystal bottle and tipped the contents of it into a plant pot. Then she quickly filled the bottle back up with water, and put it back in the golden box.

The next day, the queen put the usual three drops of potion into the king's silver goblet but, of course, it was just harmless water and her power over the good king was broken.

That day, the wicked queen had locked three children from the village in the castle dungeon for no good reason. When the children's parents came to complain to the king, he couldn't believe his ears.

"My wife would never do such a thing," he told them. But nevertheless, he went to check for himself and was shocked to find the children there.

When the brave little maid heard what had happened, she rushed off to see the king. She told him all about what she had seen in the wicked queen's room and about the magic potion. The king was furious to hear how the people of his kingdom had been treated. He discovered that the wicked queen was really a witch in disguise, and he banished her from his kingdom forever.

He, and his subjects, lived happily ever after.

This Old Man

This old man, he played one;
He played knick-knack on my drum.
With a knick-knack, paddy whack,
Give a dog a bone; this old man came rolling home.

This old man, he played two;
He played knick-knack on my shoe.
With a knick-knack, paddy whack,
Give a dog a bone; this old man came rolling home.

This old man, he played three;
He played knick-knack on my knee.
With a knick-knack, paddy whack,
Give a dog a bone; this old man came rolling home.

This old man, he played four;
He played knick-knack on my door.
With a knick-knack, paddy whack,
Give a dog a bone; this old man came rolling home.

This old man, he played five;
He played knick-knack on my hive.
With a knick-knack, paddy whack,
Give a dog a bone; this old man came rolling home.

My Favourite Chair

My favourite chair is small like me,
I sit on it to watch TV.
And sometimes when I read a book
I take my chair into a nook
And sit there while I turn the pages,
I often stay like that for ages.

I know that, as the years go by,
I will grow up very high,
But my chair will stay as small
As it is now (chairs don't grow tall).
But for now I fit just right,
So I'll continue to sit tight!

A Magical Birthday!

Emily had been crossing off the days on her calendar for weeks, and now her special day was finally here – it was her birthday at long last!

"Wake up!" called Emily, rushing into her parents' room. But when she got there, a sorry sight met her eyes. Her mother was propped up in bed with a nose as red as a radish!

"A…a…atishoo! Happy birthday darling," sniffled her mum. "I've caught a bug. We'll have to cancel your party I'm afraid. You won't be able to get it ready all by yourself."

But Emily insisted that she wanted to at least try.

"OK," said her mum, doubtfully. "You can give it a go."

Emily put on her best party dress and set to work. She laid a pretty cloth on the table and emptied crisps, biscuits and sausage rolls onto plates.

Now for the cake! This was the trickiest part. Emily stirred together the ingredients and tipped the mixture into a cake tin.

Knowing that she was too young to use the oven, Emily skipped next door to fetch her neighbour, Mrs Kindly, to help her.

"Well I never, you have been busy!" gasped Mrs Kindly when she saw the state of the kitchen. There were splodges of cake batter all over the place and her lovely party dress

was covered in blobs of food.

"Oh, no!" sobbed Emily. "My birthday is ruined!" The sad birthday girl covered her face with her hands and began to cry. All of a sudden, there was a flash of light which made her look up. Emily could hardly believe her eyes but... yes, it was true! Her lovely old neighbour had sprouted wings and was holding a magic wand!

"I am your fairy godmother!" exclaimed the transformed Mrs Kindly. "Everybody has one, although they don't always know it. We're supposed to stay secret, but this is an emergency!"

With a few waves of her magic wand, Emily's fairy godmother put everything in order. A beautiful iced cake stood in the centre of a sparkling table of party food, and Emily's dress was as good as new!

The party was a huge success and, after the guests had left, Emily rushed into her mother's room to tell her all about it.

"Mrs Kindly is certainly a helpful woman," laughed Mum. "But fairy godmother might be stretching it a bit far!"

Whether her mother believed her or not, Emily knew that this had been her best birthday ever!

A Was an Apple Pie

A was an apple pie,
B bit it,
C cut it,
D dealt it,
E eyed it,
F fought for it,
G got it,
H had it,
I inspected it,
J jumped for it,
K kept it,

L longed for it,
M mourned for it,
N nodded at it,
O opened it,
P peeped in it,
Q quartered it,
R ran for it,
S stole it,
T took it,
U upset it,
V viewed it,
W wanted it,
X, Y, Z,
All wished for
a piece in hand.

The Golden Goose

Once there were three brothers. The older brothers thought the youngest, named Peter, was silly, and took little notice of him. The older two brothers cut wood for a living, but they thought Peter was too silly to work with them.

One day, Peter decided to try cutting wood. His brothers teased him when he set off. "Don't cut off your leg by mistake," they called after him.

When Peter was about to strike his first blow at a tree, a little man appeared. "I am hungry and thirsty," said the man. "Will you share your food with me?"

Peter had only some bread and water with him, but gladly shared it with the little man. In return the man gave Peter some advice. "Cut down that old tree over there," he said, pointing to a dead tree. "You'll find something interesting sitting in its roots that will change your life."

So Peter swung his axe at the tree and chopped it down. He was amazed to find a golden goose sitting on the stump. He picked up the goose and set off with it under his arm.

After a while, Peter felt sleepy and lay down for a nap. While he dozed, three girls passed by and, seeing the golden goose, tried to take golden feathers from it. But as soon as they touched the golden goose, they found they were stuck

fast. When Peter woke up, he just walked on, ignoring the girls
who were stuck.

Soon Peter passed a priest who wanted to touch the goose,
but he became stuck to the girls. Soon the priest's assistant
and some farm hands also became stuck. But Peter paid no
attention to them and just kept on walking.

After a while, Peter walked past a royal castle. A princess
was sitting in the castle, and when she saw Peter, she laughed
and laughed. She laughed so hard that, after a while her
father, the king, came out to see what was so funny. The king
had never seen his daughter so happy, she was usually a sad
little thing, so he allowed her to marry Peter.

"I hope I won't have to marry all these people who are
stuck to you as well," laughed the princess. Peter suddenly
noticed the procession of people behind him. He looked so
surprised that the princess started laughing all over again.

As soon as Peter put down the goose, all the people who
were stuck were suddenly released.

Peter and his princess lived happily ever after, and his
brothers never thought he was silly again.

Little Bo-Peep

Little Bo-Peep has lost her sheep,
And doesn't know where to find them;
Leave them alone,
And they'll come home,
Wagging their tails behind them.

Mary Had a Little Lamb

Mary had a little lamb,
Its fleece was white as snow;
And everywhere that Mary went
The lamb was sure to go.
It followed her to school one day,
Which was against the rule;
It made the children laugh and play
To see a lamb at school.

Baa, Baa, Black Sheep

Baa, baa, black sheep, have you any wool?
Yes sir, yes sir, three bags full.
One for the master,
And one for the dame,
And one for the little boy
Who lives down the lane.

Cock-a-Doodle-Doo!

Cock-a-doodle-doo!
My dame has lost her shoe!
My master's lost his fiddling stick,
And doesn't know what to do.

Little Boy Blue

Little Boy Blue, come blow your horn.
The sheep's in the meadow,
The cow's in the corn.
Where is the boy who looks after the sheep?
He's under a haycock, fast asleep.
Will you wake him?
No, not I, for if I do, he's sure to cry.

Goosey, Goosey, Gander

Goosey, goosey, gander,
Whither do you wander?
Upstairs and downstairs
And in my lady's chamber.
There I met an old man
Who would not say his prayers,
So I took him by the left leg,
And threw him down the stairs.

The Ugly Duckling

Mummy Duck was waiting for her new eggs to hatch. All of a sudden, one of the eggs made a tapping noise. Tap! Tap!

Mummy Duck called to the other ducks.

"My eggs are hatching. Come and see!"

One by one, out popped five chirpy little ducklings.

"What sweet little ducklings!" everyone sighed. Mummy Duck beamed with pride. Cheep! Cheep!

But the biggest egg of all still hadn't opened. And Mummy was sure she had only laid five eggs...

Craaaak! Just then the final egg burst open and out tumbled the last duckling. Everyone peered at it closely.

"Oh!" gasped Mummy Duck.

"Ooh!" spluttered the other ducks.

"What an ugly duckling!" quacked an old duck.

"He's not ugly!" said Mummy Duck. "He's special."

The ugly duckling hid his head under his wing.

The next day Mummy Duck took all her little ducks to the farmyard.

"Hello everyone,"

she called to the animals. "Meet my ducklings."

The five yellow ducklings proudly puffed out their pretty feathers.

"Ah," sighed the animals, "what lovely ducklings."

The ugly duckling waddled forward. "Hello," he said.

There was a moment's silence.

Then...

"He's so **grey!**" said all the animals who saw him.

"He's so **clumsy!**" mooed a cow.

"He's so **big!**" squawked a hen.

The ugly duckling sank to the ground as large teardrops rolled down his long beak and splashed on the ground.

The ugly duckling felt all alone. "Nobody wants me," he whispered. "I'd be better off running away." With a breaking heart, the poor little duckling waddled across the meadow, leaving the farm and his family far behind him.

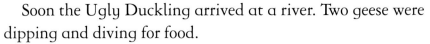

Soon the Ugly Duckling arrived at a river. Two geese were dipping and diving for food.

"Excuse me," the ugly ducking began bravely, "have you seen any ducklings like me?" The geese shook their heads.

"You're the strangest looking duckling we've ever seen," they honked. The Ugly Duckling waddled away as fast as he could. He kept going until he came to a large lake.

"If nobody wants me, then I'll just hide here forever," sniffed the Ugly Duckling, making himself a little nest among the reeds.

All through the long winter, the ugly duckling hid in his lonely clump of reeds, ashamed to show his face. But spring soon arrived and he couldn't help but peer out of his hiding place to look at the pretty landscape.

A graceful swan paddled into view and the ugly duckling backed away, afraid he would be teased. Instead, the swan

swam up to him and nudged him gently with its beak.

"Why are you hiding here?" asked the swan, kindly. "Come and join the rest of us."

The ugly duckling was so shocked he almost fell into the water. Surely the swan must be talking to someone else. But just as the ugly duckling stood up, he caught sight of his reflection in the lake. He stopped, stared and gasped in amazement. His grey feathers were now snowy white!

Just then a family of five young ducks waddled along the riverbank with their mother.

"Look at that beautiful swan!" they quacked, pointing at the ugly duckling.

Mummy Duck recognised her little ugly duckling at once. "I always knew he was special," she quacked.

The Ugly Duckling held his head high on his elegant neck, ruffled his beautiful white feathers and proudly paddled away after his new friends.

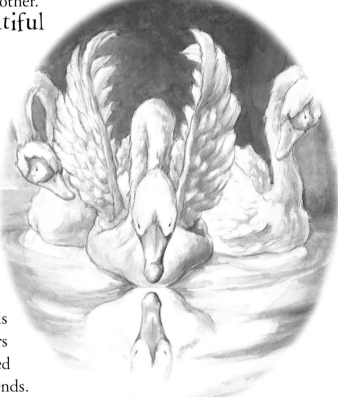

Snow White

One snowy day, a queen sat sewing by her window. She accidently pricked her finger with the needle, and three drops of blood fell on the snow. The queen looked at the bright red blood on the white snow, against the black wood of the window frame, and thought: "I wish I had a child with lips as **red** as blood, skin as **white** as snow and hair as **black** as ebony wood!"

Some time after that, the queen gave birth to a little girl with deep red lips, snowy-white skin and glossy hair as black as ebony. She called her Snow White.

Sadly, the queen died, and the king married again. His new wife was beautiful, but cruel and selfish. She had a magic mirror, and every day she looked into it and asked:

"Mirror, mirror, on the wall, who is the fairest one of all?" And every day the mirror replied, *"You, O Queen are the fairest of them all."*

But as Snow White grew up, she grew more beautiful. And so, one morning, the queen's mirror said to her: *"You, O Queen, are fair, it's true. But Snow White is much fairer than you."*

In a jealous rage, the queen called her huntsman. "Take Snow White into the forest and kill her," she told him.

The huntsman took Snow White to the edge of the forest, but he could not bear to hurt her. "Run away, child," he said.

Poor, frightened Snow White! She was all alone, lost in the forest, running for her life.

Towards nightfall, Snow White came to a little cottage deep in the woods. She knocked softly, but there was no answer, so she let herself in. Inside, Snow White found a table and seven tiny chairs. Upstairs there were seven little beds.

"I'm so tired," she yawned, and she lay down and fell asleep.

A while later, she woke with a start. Seven little men were standing round her bed.

"Who are you?" she asked them.

"We are the seven dwarfs who live here," said one of the little men. "We work in the mines all day. Who are you?"

"I am Snow White," she replied, and she told them her sad story. The dwarfs felt sorry for Snow White. "If you cook and clean for us," said the eldest dwarf, "you can stay here, and we will keep you safe."

Snow White gratefully agreed. When they left for work the next morning, the dwarfs made Snow White promise not to go out, or open the door, or speak to anyone.

Meanwhile, the queen was back at her magic mirror. But she was shocked by what it told her:

"You are the fairest here, it's true, but there is someone fairer than you. Deep in the forest, in a cosy den, Snow White lives with seven little men."

"What?" shrieked the queen. "Snow White is alive?" The queen, who was really a wicked witch, brewed a deadly potion and **poisoned** a rosy red apple. Then, disguising herself as an old woman, she set out for the seven dwarfs' cottage.

Snow White was busy in the kitchen when she saw an old woman at the window. "Try my lovely red apples!" the old woman croaked. And she handed the poisoned apple to Snow White.

She took a big bite... and fell down **dead.** The queen hurried home to her magic mirror. At last it gave her the answer she wanted: *"You, O Queen, are the fairest of them all!"*

The dwarfs wept bitterly when they found Snow White dead. They didn't want to bury her and so they put her in a glass coffin. They watched over her, day and night.

One day a prince came riding through the forest. When he saw Snow White, he instantly fell in love with her.

"Please let me take the coffin back to my castle," he begged the dwarfs, and they agreed.

As the prince's servants lifted the coffin, one of them stumbled, and the piece of apple that was stuck in Snow White's throat came loose. Snow White opened her eyes.

Snow White looked into the prince's kind, gentle eyes, and she knew she loved him, too.

And so they were married, with the dwarfs beside them. They all lived happily together in the prince's castle for the rest of their long lives.

Mermaid Dreams

I wish I was a mermaid
Swimming beneath the sea.
My pet would be a dolphin
Who'd swim along with me.

We'd play among the coral,
And in and out of caves.
If we felt quite brave enough,
We'd peep above the waves.

Perhaps my wish will not come true,
I'll have to wait and see.
But if you ever see a mermaid,
Please wave – it might be me!

The Magic Pie

Once upon a time, a kind woman baked a pie and shared it with her friends. But when she went to wash the empty dish – she couldn't **believe** her eyes! The pie was still there as if it had just come out of the oven. The next day she shared the pie with some hungry travellers and, when she went to wash the dish, she saw once again that the pie was still there.

News of the magic pie spread, and many hungry people came to be fed by the kind woman's **magic** pie.

A **greedy** king heard about the magic pie and wanted it for himself. He sent his soldiers to fetch the pie, and they took it to the royal kitchen. A butler placed the pie beneath a silver dome and went straight to the king to present it to him. The king licked his lips and lifted the dome... but the pie was **gone!** All that remained of it was a pile of mouldy dust.

The king vowed never to eat pie again and, as for the kind woman? Well, she just baked another pie!

Hickety Pickety

Hickety Pickety, my black hen,
She lays eggs for gentlemen;
Sometimes nine, and sometimes ten,
Hickety Pickety, my black hen!

Marking Time

Tick! Tock!
That's the clock
Marking time for me.
Every tick
And every tock,
Sets each second free.

Hickory, Dickory, Dock

Hickory, dickory, dock,
The mouse ran up the clock.
The clock struck one,
The mouse ran down,
Hickory, dickory, dock.

I Had a Little Hen

I had a little hen, the prettiest ever seen,
She washed up the dishes, and kept the house clean.
She went to the mill to fetch me some flour,
And always got home in less than an hour.
She baked me my bread, she brewed me my ale,
She sat by the fire and told a fine tale!

Three Blind Mice

Three blind mice, three blind mice,
See how they run, see how they run!
They all ran after the farmer's wife,
Who cut off their tails with a carving knife,
Did you ever see such a thing in your life
As three blind mice?

Pussy Cat, Pussy Cat

Pussy cat, pussy cat, where have you been?
I've been to London to visit the Queen.
Pussy cat, pussy cat, what did you there?
I frightened a little mouse under her chair.

The Elves and the Shoemaker

Once, there was a shoemaker and his wife who were very poor. The day came when the shoemaker had only one piece of leather left, so he cut out one last pair of shoes and went to bed with a heavy heart.

That night, two **helpful** elves came out to play. They saw the leather, and sewed it very neatly into a pair of shoes.

The next morning, the shoemaker came downstairs and was **amazed** to find the finished shoes. "What delicate work!" he said.

Just then, a woman came into the shoe shop. When she saw the shoes with their beautiful stitching, she tried them on and they fitted perfectly. "These shoes are just right," she said, and gave the shoemaker twice the money he usually got. The shoemaker had enough money to buy a big piece of leather.

That evening, the shoemaker cut out some boots.

During the night, the two elves came out to work again. They saw the leather and sewed a beautiful pair of boots.

The next morning, the shoemaker was happy to find the boots. "What wonderful work!" he said.

Just then, a man came into the shoe shop. He took off his shoes and tried on the boots. "These boots are just right," he said. He paid handsomely for them, so the shoemaker bought a **bigger** piece of leather, which he used to cut out a pair of shoes and a pair of boots.

"Who is making the shoes and boots?" asked the shoemaker's wife. "Let's see if we can find out!"

When it was time for bed, the shoemaker and his wife hid. Soon, the elves came out and sewed the shoes and the boots.

"What **kind** elves," the shoemaker said to his wife. "How can we thank them?"

"Let's make them some shoes!" said the shoemaker's wife.

So the shoemaker got his **finest** piece of leather and they made two pairs of tiny shoes.

That night, the shoemaker and his wife hid, and watched as the elves tried on the tiny shoes – they fitted **perfectly!**

The two elves danced happily away into the night.

After the elves had gone, lots of people came to buy shoes and boots.

The shoemaker and his wife were never poor again.

Fairy Daisy

Daisy was the most playful little fairy in Fairyland. She was as fresh as a spring morning and always **giggling.**

The smaller fairies all loved playing with Daisy. She always thought of games that were such fun!

"Come and play with us," called three little fairies to Daisy one day. Daisy had just been given her first **magic** wand and was busy practising how to use it.

"Look at me," giggled Daisy. "I'm making magic flowers grow." The three little fairies ran up to their favourite fairy to take a closer look. "Can we have a go?" they asked.

"You're too little to use a magic wand," Daisy told them. "But I can think of a game that will be great fun!"

Daisy waved her new wand over one of the little fairies and there was a **magical** puff of green mist. When the mist cleared, the other two fairies both laughed to see that Daisy had turned their friend a lovely shade of **pea green!**

"Me next! Me next!" the other two fairies called. Daisy used her new magic wand to turn the little fairies into all the colours of the **rainbow.** It was terrific fun and they all laughed until they were out of breath.

They had all been so busy playing, that nobody had noticed how late it had got. The little fairies had to go home for their lunch. "You can change us back now," they said.

But when Daisy tried to change them back to their usual colour, she couldn't make her spell work. First she made them **spotty** and, when she tried again, she made them **stripy!**

"Oh no!" cried the playful fairy. "Whatever will your mothers say?"

Daisy took her little friends home and explained what had happened. Luckily their mothers were better at using magic wands than Daisy was, and turned them all back to normal. Daisy didn't get into too much **trouble,** but from then on she was known as Whoops-a-Daisy!

I See the Moon

I see the moon and the moon sees me.
God bless the moon and God bless me.

Go to Sleep

Go to sleep my baby,
Close your pretty eyes,
Angels are above us,
Peeping through the skies.

Great big moon is shining,
Stars begin to peep.
Time for little babies
All to go to sleep.

Old Mother Hubbard

Old Mother Hubbard
Went to the cupboard,
To get her poor doggie a bone;
But when she got there
The cupboard was bare,
So her poor little doggie had none.

Once I Saw a Little Bird

Once I saw a little bird
Come hop, hop, hop;
So I cried, "Little bird,
Will you STOP, STOP, STOP?"
I was going to the window,
To say, "How do you do?"
But he shook his little tail,
And far away he flew.

Dickery Dare

Dickery, dickery, dare,
The pig flew up in the air.
The man in brown
Soon brought him down!
Dickery, dickery, dare.

I Had a Little Hobby-Horse

I had a little hobby-horse,
And it was dapple grey;
Its head was made of pea-straw,
Its tail was made of hay.

I sold it to an old woman
For a copper groat;
And I'll not sing my song again
Without another coat.

Higglety, Pigglety, Pop!

Higglety, pigglety, pop!
The dog has eaten the mop;
The pig's in a hurry,
The cat's in a flurry,
Higglety, pigglety, POP!

Horsie, Horsie

Horsie, horsie, don't you stop,
Just let your hooves go clippety clop;
Your tail goes swish,
And the wheels go round;
Giddy-up, you're homeward bound!

A Sailor Went to Sea

A sailor went to sea, sea, sea.
To see what he could see, see, see.
But all that he could see, see, see,
Was the bottom of the deep blue sea, sea, sea.

Have you ever, ever, ever,
In your long-legged life,
Met a long-legged sailor
With a long-legged wife?

No, I never, never, never,
In my long-legged life,
Met a long-legged sailor
With a long-legged wife!

Have you ever, ever, ever,
In your pigeon-toed life,
Met a pigeon-toed sailor
With a pigeon-toed wife?

No, I never, never, never,
In my pigeon-toed life,
Met a pigeon-toed sailor
With a pigeon-toed wife!

This is the Way

This is the way we wash our hands,
Wash our hands, wash our hands.
This is the way we wash our hands
On a cold and frosty morning.

This is the way we wash our face,
Wash our face, wash our face.
This is the way we wash our face
On a cold and frosty morning.

This is the way we brush our teeth,
Brush our teeth, brush our teeth.
This is the way we brush our teeth
On a cold and frosty morning.

This is the way we comb our hair,
Comb our hair, comb our hair.
This is the way we comb our hair
On a cold and frosty morning.

This is the way we wave goodbye,
Wave goodbye, wave goodbye.
This is the way we wave goodbye
On a cold and frosty morning.

The Pobble

The Pobble who has no toes,
Had once as many as we.
When they said, "Some day you may lose them all,"
He replied "Fish, fiddle-de-dee!"
And his Aunt Jobiska made him drink
Lavender water tinged with pink,
For she said, "The World in general knows
There's nothing so good for a Pobble's toes!"

The Pobble who has no toes
Swam across the Bristol Channel,
But before he set out he wrapped his nose
In a piece of scarlet flannel.
For his Aunt Jobiska said, "No harm
Can come to his toes if his nose is warm.
And it's perfectly known that a Pobble's toes
Are safe, provided he minds his nose!"

But before he touched the shore,
The shore of the Bristol Channel,
A sea-green porpoise carried away
His wrapper of scarlet flannel.
And when he came to observe his feet,
Formerly garnished with toes so neat,
His face at once became forlorn,
On perceiving that all his toes were gone!

The Pobble who has no toes
Was placed in a friendly bark,
And they rowed him back, and carried him up
To his Aunt Jobiska's Park.
And she made him a feast at his earnest wish
Of eggs and buttercups fried with fish.
And she said, "It's a fact the whole world knows,
That Pobbles are happier without their toes!"

Princess in Peril

There was once a happy-go-lucky princess whose name was Wanda.

One hot summer's day, Princess Wanda went for a ride on Snowy, her favourite horse. The sun shone brightly and, as she rode along, Princess Wanda sang happily to the rhythm of Snowy's hooves as they clip-clopped along the path. Soon, the palace where she lived was just a speck in the distance and the sun was going down, but still the carefree princess rode on.

Feeling adventurous, she and Snowy rode into some woods. The air was cooler under the tree tops, and Princess Wanda climbed down off her horse and sat beneath the shady branches while Snowy grazed lazily on some grass.

Suddenly there was a loud cackle and a witch jumped out from behind a nearby tree, as if from nowhere. Snowy was so frightened that she bolted away, back down the path and towards her home at the palace.

"Ha, ha!" cackled the wicked witch as she pointed her magic wand at the frightened princess. "You are my prisoner now!" And as the wand cast its magical light over Princess Wanda, she found that she was unable to resist as the wicked witch led her to a castle and locked her in a room, high up in a tower.

Then, the wicked witch took the golden locket from around Princess Wanda's neck. "This will do very nicely," she cackled. "I will send it to your father as proof that you are my prisoner. He will have to give me lots of gold if he wants his precious daughter back!"

Back at Princess Wanda's palace, Snowy had returned without her and everyone was very worried.

"Where can my little princess be?" sobbed her poor mother.

When the king and queen received Princess Wanda's golden necklace with a message from the wicked witch, the king wanted to send his army out to fetch her. But the royal wizard, Enigmo, warned the king that the witch's magic was very powerful, and told him that even an entire army would be no good against her powerful magic.

"Don't worry, I'll find Princess Wanda and bring her back home," promised Enigmo.

He set off right away, flying on the back of his enchanted dragon. Enigmo and the dragon flew away from the royal palace and over the shady woods, determined to find the lost princess and defeat the witch. They flew for many hours, scanning the wooded ground beneath them, but they could not see any trace of the princess or the witch.

"I felt sure that the witch's castle was in these woods," sighed Enigmo. Just as the young wizard and his dragon were about to fly away, the wizard heard a **beautiful** sound. An enchanting melody floated up into the air, and Enigmo recognized it at once.

"It's Princess Wanda!" Enigmo explained to his dragon. "The witch must have put an invisibility spell on the castle to stop us finding her, but her magic wasn't enough to stop

Princess Wanda's beautiful voice from escaping."

Following the lovely sound, Enigmo and his dragon swooped down through the invisibility barrier until they could see the castle, with Princess Wanda waving to them from the tower.

"I'll be back for you very soon," called Enigmo to Princess Wanda, as she greeted him from the window. "But first I must defeat the wicked witch so that she can never work her evil magic again!"

The dragon glided gently to the ground. Enigmo climbed down from his scaly back and set off to find the witch.

Enigmo crept into the castle, searching for the witch. He peeped around a door and saw the witch cackling to herself and dancing about.

"When the king brings me his gold, I will be rich. I will make that foolish king my prisoner, too, and then I will be in charge of everything," she said.

Enigmo mumbled a spell and, before the witch had time to notice him, she was transformed into a frog, and her magic wand clattered to the ground.

"That wicked witch can do no more harm now," Enigmo told the princess, as he helped her up onto the dragon's back.

When Princess Wanda arrived home, the king and queen were delighted. They threw a fantastic party to celebrate, and Enigmo and his dragon were the guests of honour.

Sippity Sup, Sippity Sup

Sippity sup, sippity sup,
Bread and milk from a china cup.
Bread and milk from a bright silver spoon
Made of a piece of the bright silver moon.
Sippity sup, sippity sup,
Sippity, sippity sup.

Vintery, Mintery

Vintery, mintery, cuttery, corn,
Apple seed and apple thorn;
Wire, briar, limber lock,
Three geese in a flock.
One flew east, and one flew west,
And one flew over the cuckoo's nest.

It's Raining, It's Pouring

It's raining, it's pouring,
The old man is snoring.
He went to bed and he bumped his head,
And couldn't get up in the morning.

There Was a Crooked Man

There was a crooked man and he walked a crooked mile,
He found a crooked sixpence upon a crooked stile;
He bought a crooked cat,
Which caught a crooked mouse,
And they all lived together in a little crooked house.

Michael Finnegan

There was an old man called Michael Finnegan.
He grew whiskers on his chinnegan.
The wind came out and blew them in again.
Poor old Michael Finnegan.
Begin again.

Diddle, Diddle, Dumpling

Diddle, diddle, dumpling, my son John,
Went to bed with his trousers on;
One shoe off, and one shoe on,
Diddle, diddle, dumpling, my son John.

Rosie and Bluebell

Rosie and Bluebell went out one day,
Gathering flowers they found on their way.
Petals of yellow, purple and pink,
Bunched up together as quick as a wink.

"Mine are for Mummy," said Bluebell to Rosie,
"She'll be so pleased with this lovely posy."
"Mine are for Grandma," said Rosie to Bluebell,
"She will so love the nice way that they smell."

Bluebell and Rosie skipped home happily,
Holding the posies they'd picked with such glee.
"Hello!" they called as they ran through the door,
Clutching their handfuls of petals galore.

"Thank you so much!" said Grandma to Rosie,
As she handed over her beautiful posy.
"Gorgeous!" said Mummy, hugging Bluebell,
"What a truly beautiful smell!"

The Moonlit Moors

The heat has lifted from the land,
The dusky light is dim.
The moon is rising in the sky;
The night is moving in.

Rabbits raise their timid heads
Above the moonlit moors,
They sniff the air and wonder
If it's safe to go outdoors.

The heather glows so softly
In the silvery twilight,
Beautiful, beneath the moon
Which shines its gentle light.

There's no place I'd rather be
At this special time,
For when the moon is on the moors,
I feel the world is mine.

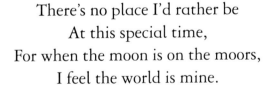

The Singing Princess

There was once a princess called Melody who would not stop singing. She sang all day and half of the night. Although she had a pretty voice, the whole palace was fed up with it and begged her to stop. But the princess just went on singing.

The king decided to build Princess Melody a little house in the palace grounds where she could sing to her heart's content without disturbing anyone.

One day, the princess was singing her heart out and her song went soaring into the sky. A travelling knight heard the tune and began to sing along.

"What beautiful music!" thought the knight.

He rode on and the song became louder as he got nearer to the princess.

As the princess sang she became aware of another voice joining in. Together the two voices merged as one and sounded beautiful. Before long, the two singers found themselves face to face.

"I'm Princess Melody," sang the princess.

"I'm Sir Harmony," replied the Knight.

The two singers fell in love and were married. They made beautiful music together and lived happily ever after.

Free as a Bird

Lucky birds, they fly so free,
I wish that I could also be
Way up, soaring in the air -
I'd fly around, without a care.

If only I could take to flight
I'd flutter on the breeze, so light.
Although I don't have feathered wings,
I can fly upon my swing.

Swinging high, swinging low,
Up and down, to and fro.
The wind is blowing through my hair,
I'm free as a bird, light as the air.

I swing my legs, and push so high,
Perhaps I'll even touch the sky!
I can fly so high that soon,
I might even reach the moon!

Aiken Drum

There was a man lived in the moon,
Lived in the moon, lived in the moon,
There was a man lived in the moon,
And his name was Aiken Drum.

And he played upon a ladle,
A ladle, a ladle,
He played upon a ladle,
And his name was Aiken Drum.

And his hat was made of good cream cheese,
Of good cream cheese, of good cream cheese,
And his hat was made of good cream cheese,
And his name was Aiken Drum.

And his coat was made of good roast beef,
Of good roast beef, of good roast beef,
And his coat was made of good roast beef,
And his name was Aiken Drum.

And his buttons were made of penny loaves,
Of penny loaves, of penny loaves,
And his buttons were made of penny loaves,
And his name was Aiken Drum.

Five Fat Sausages

Five fat sausages sizzling in the pan,
All of a sudden one went **bang!**

Four fat sausages sizzling in the pan,
All of a sudden one went **bang!**

Three fat sausages sizzling in the pan,
All of a sudden one went **bang!**

Two fat sausages sizzling in the pan,
All of a sudden one went **bang!**

One fat sausage sizzling in the pan,
All of a sudden it went **bang!**

And there were no sausages left!

The Musicians of Bremen

Once upon a time, a farmer had a donkey which was old and unfit and he wanted to get rid of it. The donkey, who was a clever beast, decided to run away and become a musician. So he set off for the town of Bremen.

The donkey hadn't walked far, when he found a dog lying on the road, **panting and gasping** to get his breath.

"Why are you panting so hard?" asked the donkey.

"Ah," puffed the hound. "As I'm so old, my master wanted to get rid of me, so I ran away."

"Hey, why don't you join me?" said the donkey. "I'm going to Bremen to become a musician."

The old dog quickly agreed, and they went on together.

After they had walked a short distance, they heard a cat **meowing** sorrowfully.

"Oh dear," said the donkey. "What's wrong with you?"

"As I'm too old to catch mice, my mistress wanted to get rid of me, so I ran away. " he said.

"Come with us to Bremen. You sing beautifully and will make a fine musician." said the donkey. The cat thought this sounded like a splendid idea and decided to join them.

They set off again and soon met a cockerel. **"Cock-a-doodle-doo!"** he crowed. "My mistress wants to feed me to her guests," he continued, sadly.

"We can't let that happen," said the donkey. "You'd better come with us. We're off to town to become musicians. You could sing with us." The cockerel quickly agreed, and all four carried on down the road.

That evening, the donkey and dog settled down beneath a tree. The cat settled on a low branch. And the cockerel flew to the top of the tree, where it was safest. Before settling down, the cockerel looked around and saw a light in the distance.

"There's a house not far from here," he called to his new friends. "I can see lights."

So, instead of sleeping beneath the tree, they made their way to the house, which was glowing with lights.

The donkey, being the biggest, peered through the window.

"What do you see?" asked the cockerel.

"A table covered with good things to eat and drink, and thieves sitting around enjoying themselves."

"This would be a perfect place for us to live," said the cat. And they all came up with a plan to get rid of the robbers.

The animals climbed on top of each other and began to perform their music:

"Eeee-ooar!" the donkey brayed.

"Woof! Woof!" the dog barked.

"Meow! Meow!" the cat mewed.

"Cock-a-doodle-doo!" the cockerel crowed.

Then they all burst in through the window, scattering the robbers in all directions. The thieves, who thought that some horrible monster had come for them, scampered away as fast as they could.

The four animals sat down at the thieves' table and ate, and ate.

Then they turned out the lights and searched for a bed. The donkey lay down on some straw in the yard. The dog lay on the mat beside the door. The cat curled up in front of the fire. And the cockerel perched on top of the chimney. They all fell swiftly to sleep.

But the thieves hadn't run far and, when they saw that the house was dark, one of them went back to investigate.

The thief found the house still and quiet, so he went into the kitchen to light a candle. When he saw the **fiery** eyes of the cat glittering in the fireplace, he thought they were hot coals and held some paper to them to get a light. The cat was **furious** and flew at his face. The thief ran for the door, but the dog, who lay there, sprang up and bit his leg. The injured thief raced across the yard, where the donkey kicked him smartly on his backside. Then the cockerel, who had been awakened by the noise, crowed with all his might. The terrified thief ran back to the other thieves.

"There's a **terrible** witch in the house," he told his friends. "She spat at me and scratched my face with her long claws. Then there was a man by the door who stabbed me in the leg with a knife. And a monster in the yard who beat me with a wooden club. And on the roof there's a demon judge, who called out, 'COOK THE CROOK DO.' So I ran away while I still could."

After that night, the robbers never again dared to return to the house. And it suited the four musicians so well that they decided to stay. I expect that they are still there now.

What Are Little Boys Made of?

What are little boys made of?
What are little boys made of?
Slugs and snails,
And puppy-dogs' tails,
That's what little boys are made of.

Tweedledum and Tweedledee

Tweedledum and Tweedledee
Agreed to have a battle;
For Tweedledum said Tweedledee
Had spoiled his nice new rattle.
Just then flew down a monstrous crow,
As black as a tar-barrel,
Which frightened both the heroes so,
They quite forgot their quarrel.

Robin and Richard

Robin and Richard were two pretty men,
They lay in bed till the clock struck ten;
Then up starts Robin, and looks at the sky,
"Oh! Oh! brother Richard, the sun's very high,
You go before with bottle and bag,
And I'll follow after on little Jack Nag."

What Are Little Girls Made of?

What are little girls made of?
What are little girls made of?
Sugar and spice,
And all things nice,
That's what little girls are made of.

Miss Mary Mack

Miss Mary Mack, all dressed in black,
With silver buttons all down her back,
She asked her mother for fifty pence,
To see the elephant jump the fence.
They jumped so high, they touched the sky,
And didn't come back 'til the fourth of July.

Little Nancy Etticoat

Little Nancy Etticoat, in a white petticoat,
And a red rose.
The longer she stands,
The shorter she grows.

What is she? A candle!

Angel Lily

How Sophia wished she could do cartwheels. Her friends Abby and Katie could both do fantastic cartwheels. But try as she might, she just **couldn't** get it right. After a while Sophia gave up trying and went to sit beneath the willow tree.

"I wish I could be like my friends," she said out loud. As she spoke, there was a flash of light and a **beautiful** lady appeared. Sophia was very surprised. The lady had soft, downy wings and a ring of light **shimmered** above her head, but Sophia didn't feel afraid at all.

"Who are you?" asked Sophia shyly.

"My name's Lily, I'm your guardian angel," replied the lady. "Come with me, I want to show you some things."

Angel Lily took Sophia to where her friends were playing.

"Look, I've got a guardian angel!" said Sophia. But Abby and Katie didn't reply.

"Why are my friends ignoring me?" said Sophia.

"I'm your personal guardian angel, so you are the only one who can see me. And when you're with me,

"no one can see or hear you either," Angel Lily explained.

Sophia was busy thinking about how strange it was to be invisible, when she heard a yelp. She span around and saw Abby sitting on the grass, with her skipping rope tangled around her ankles. Abby got up, giggling.

"Abby tries her best but she's not great at skipping," said Angel Lily. Angel Lily turned Sophia around. Katie was trying to throw her ball through a basketball hoop, but she wasn't having much luck.

"Katie is wonderful at cartwheels, but not at basketball," said Angel Lily as Katie's ball bounced off the net. "All anyone can do is to try their best," smiled Angel Lily.

Sophia was thinking about this when she realised she was alone. Angel Lily had completely vanished. "Maybe she was never here at all," thought Sophia.

Feeling happy again, Sophia ran to her friends and tried a cartwheel. She didn't wobble or fall over, but stayed there on her hands.

"Wow," cried Abby. "What a fantastic handstand!"

Sophia laughed happily. It seemed that she was good at something, after all.

The Prince and the Dragon

There was a queen who would have lived happily with her husband the king, had it not been for a fierce **dragon** that terrorised their kingdom.

When the queen gave birth to a beautiful baby boy, she was afraid that the dragon would find the baby and eat him.

The king told his wife to take the child out into the woods and hide him, so she set off with the baby in her arms.

After a while, the queen came to a little cottage. She knocked on the door which was answered by a little old woman.

Although the woman was very old, she happily agreed to look after the baby boy as she was also very lonely. So the sad queen left her precious baby and went back to her husband.

"When the dragon is slain our boy can return," said the king, trying to comfort his wife. But the dragon lived on and its reign of **terror** continued.

As the years passed, the young prince grew big and brave. Although the queen had not known it, the old woman was a good witch. She grew to love the prince and, on his thirteenth birthday, she gave him a cloak, a sword and an amulet. She sent the prince back to his kingdom.

The brave young prince rode out of the woods and, almost as soon as he entered his parents' kingdom, he was met with a **fearsome** sight. A huge dragon loomed above him, breathing fire.

The prince was scared but stood his ground. He was amazed to find that the dragon's flames did not burn him because the cloak **protected** him.

The dragon came closer towards the prince who held up the amulet that the witch had given him. The sun shone right through it and a **dazzling** ray of light shot out, blinding the dragon. The prince, seeing his chance, lunged at the dragon with his sword and killed the beast with one stroke.

News soon reached the king and queen that a young man had slain the dragon, so they went to see for themselves. They instantly recognised the **brave** slayer as their own long-lost son. The prince was at last back where he belonged and there was great rejoicing throughout the kingdom.

However, when the queen went to thank the old woman in the woods, there was no sign of the little cottage or of the woman. The queen's guards were sent to look for her, but she was never found, or forgotten.

My Birthday Wish

I have a special secret wish,
One I cannot share.
I'll lock it up inside my heart;
It will be safe in there.

Nobody must find out what
Is under lock and key.
So please don't try to take a peek,
There's nothing you can see.

I'll keep it 'til my birthday,
Then I'll open up and take
My secret from its hiding place –
And wish upon my cake!

Sail Away

Sail away, for a year and a day,
To a land where dreams come true,
Lit by the moon and a blanket of stars,
Across the ocean blue.

We'll drift through silver waters
To lands we've never seen
In daylight hours, where chocolate flowers
Will taste just like a dream.

Where clouds are cotton candy,
And the sky is always blue.
What busy night-time travelling,
Will you come with us, too?

Busy Elves

When you are fast asleep at night, all tucked up in your bed,
And humans everywhere are quiet, the Elves are out instead.
They're helpful little creatures with shiny, button eyes,
They'll do odd jobs around the house to give you a surprise!

Busy Elves will tidy shelves and put your toys away,
It's not a joke, these tiny folk will watch you every day.
And when they know you've got to go to bed, I hear them say:
"No one's about, we can come out.
Hip! Hip! Hip! Hooray!"

The Shy Princess

A princess named Emily Rose
Was shy from her head to her toes,
"Come out and play,"
Other children would say.
But the princess just turned up her nose.

One day in the middle of spring
The princess had word from the king,
"We're having a party
You'd better look smartly,
I'm ordering you to join in."

The princess was red in the face
When she took up her dutiful place
Beside her royal dad,
Who was so very glad
That his daughter had not caused disgrace.

But the princess had hatched out a plan,
And when the royal dancing began,
She stood by the wall
And fooled one and all
By **hiding** behind a big fan!

The Enchanted Princess

There was once a king and queen who had such a beautiful baby daughter that the Fairy Queen came to hear of it.

"This must be a very special child indeed to be so utterly beautiful," the Fairy Queen thought to herself. And she sent three of her best fairies to give her three magical gifts. The first fairy gave her the gift of wisdom, the second gave the gift of honesty and the third gift was charity.

The king and queen had no idea how special their baby was.

By the time the princess had grown into a young lady, news of her beauty had spread far and wide. Every prince in the world wanted to marry her and, although those that came to meet her were either rich or handsome, the princess did not fall in love with any of them. The king and queen were worried.

"You have the pick of every prince in the world, surely one of them will do," sighed the perplexed queen.

"But mother," replied the princess, "I must be honest with myself. I must marry a worthy man."

Being a wise young woman, the princess realised that these princes only wanted her for her beautiful face so, when the princes came to visit her again, she made herself look ugly by placing a large **wart** from the skin of a pig on the end of her nose.

One by one the princes came to see her, but this time none proposed marriage because they were put off by the enormous wart. It was not until the last prince of all came to visit the princess that she finally met a man **worthy** of her love. This prince was from a far-off land and it had taken him many weeks to reach the princess's palace. As soon as she met him, the princess knew that he was the one, for he did not even glance at her face, but seemed to **gaze** straight into her heart.

"This is the prince I shall marry," declared the princess.

"But my dear child," replied the queen. "You cannot marry this prince, for he is **blind.**"

But because the princess had the gifts of wisdom, honesty and charity, she followed her heart and married the blind prince. She realised that true beauty comes from within and that real vision doesn't always come from the eyes. So she and her prince lived happily ever after.

Pink Fairy

If I met a fairy and she granted me three wishes,
I'd ask for lots of dainty treats upon some silver dishes.
Then I'd wish for all my friends to come and visit me,
To join a merry party with a fancy feast for tea.

Wish one and two seem like good fun, I'm sure you will agree,
But what, you may be wondering, Would be number three?
I know just what I'd ask for; I hardly have to think...
I'd like a fairy dress with glitter and, of course – pink!

The Scarecrow

In the middle of a field, where the farmer sows his crop,
You'll find my friend the scarecrow, leant against a prop.
He has a far-off, distant look within his button eyes,
And if you listen carefully, you might just hear him sigh:

"I'd like to see the big wide world, not stay here in this place
Where all the little birdies are frightened of my face.
I'd never try to harm them; I wish that they could see
That although my name is Scarecrow,
I couldn't scare a flea!"

Sweet Dreams

Princess Isabella could not sleep. Every time she rested her head on her pillow and began to doze off, she had a bad dream that **woke** her up. The little princess hadn't slept well for weeks, nor had her parents who always went to comfort her when she woke up.

"**Mummy!**" called Isabella. "I had another bad dream. It was about a monster that was coming to eat me up and I couldn't run away from it!"

And so the broken nights continued until everyone had dark circles around their eyes from lack of sleep.

"If only we could stop these bad dreams our little girl keeps having," sighed the queen one evening, as she stood by an open window. Little did she know that the Night Fairies were out and about spreading spells of kindness and happiness. There was one young fairy just outside the queen's window, who overheard what the queen had said.

The little Night Fairy knew that this was a bigger task than she could manage all by herself and so she flew off to fetch her fairy friends.

Unseen, the fairies flew into the palace and waved their **magic wands** over **everyone.** Soon there was not a sound to be heard throughout the whole palace as everyone was **sleeping peacefully,** including little Princess Isabella.

"What wonderful dreams I had last night," yawned the little princess when she woke up. "I dreamed that I was at a wonderful party in Fairyland, and that I could fly."

That night, the princess went to bed quite happily, in the hope that she would dream more **sweet** dreams, and she was not disappointed!

That very night she dreamed that she slid down a rainbow and landed in a **mermaid lagoon.** The night after that she dreamed about a wonderful orchard where the fruit was all made of chocolate.

The Night Fairies had worked their magic and Princess Isabella never had another bad dream again.

She, her parents and indeed the whole palace always slept very well!

The Queen of Hearts

The Queen of Hearts, she made some tarts
All on a summer's day.
The Knave of Hearts, he stole the tarts
And took them clean away.
The King of Hearts, called for the tarts
And beat the Knave full sore.
The Knave of Hearts, brought back the tarts
And vowed he'd steal no more.

Sing a Song of Sixpence

Sing a song of sixpence, a pocket full of rye;
Four and twenty blackbirds baked in a pie.
When the pie was opened
The birds began to sing;
Now wasn't that a dainty dish
To set before the king?
The king was in his counting house
Counting out his money;
The queen was in the parlour
Eating bread and honey.
The maid was in the garden
Hanging out the clothes,
When down came a blackbird
And pecked off her nose!

Oranges and Lemons

Oranges and lemons,
Say the bells of St Clements.
You owe me five farthings,
Say the bells of St Martins.
When will you pay me?
Say the bells of Old Bailey.
When I grow rich,
Say the bells of Shoreditch.

Betty Botter

Betty Botter bought some butter,
But she said the butter's bitter.
If I put it in my batter,
It will make my batter bitter.
But a bit of better butter
Will make my batter better.

So she bought some better butter,
Better than the bitter butter,
And she put it in her batter.
And her batter was not bitter.
So 'twas better Betty Botter
Bought a bit of better butter.

The Spooky Shipwreck

There was great excitement under the sea. There had been a storm in the night with very big waves and, when the sea had become calm again, Zippy the dolphin had found a shipwreck.

"Let's explore it!" suggested Zippy to his friends, and they all swam in through a porthole.

"It must have sunk years ago," said Zippy. "I expect the storm swept it in."

Suddenly there was a **shriek** of excitement.

"Come and see what I've found!" called Delores the jellyfish. Everyone swam over to take a look.

"Treasure!" gasped Zippy. "Perhaps this was a pirate ship."

"I hope there are no ghosts," said Delores, **wobbling** at the thought. "It's spooky here, I'm not sure that I like it."

"There are no such things as ghosts," said Zippy, doing his best to reassure her. But just then, Zippy and Delores heard a strange clicking sound. **Click! Click!** The sound was coming closer and closer towards them.

"W-w-what could it be?" stammered Delores. "It sounds like a peg-legged pirate coming this way!"

Zippy and Delores hid behind the treasure chest, shivering with fear. **Click! Click! Click!** Whatever was making the spooky sound was almost there. Bravely, Zippy peeped out from behind the treasure.

"Ha! It's only our friend Wanda the lobster, coming to see the treasure!" laughed Zippy.

Wanda admired the treasure as it glinted through the water. "It's so pretty! I wonder what we should do with it."

The sea creatures decided to ask King Neptune what they should do, and swam off to his palace.

"Treasure, eh?" boomed Neptune. "I've got too much treasure already, I don't need any more. You have my permission to do what you like with it!"

At first the sea creatures couldn't think of anything to do with their exciting find, and then Wanda had a fantastic idea. "We all had such fun playing in the shipwreck this morning, so let's open a Spooky Pirate theme park and then everyone can join in the fun!" said the little lobster, who was pink with excitement.

So the friends dressed up as pirates and invited all the creatures of the sea to come along and see the sunken ship and its treasure. And the most popular attraction at the theme park was The Clicking Peg-legged Ghost. Wanda had to click her claws so often that they got rather sore!

A Journey

If I could travel through the years, I'd like to go back when
There were no cars or aeroplanes to journey on, and then,
I'd ride upon a **carriage** that was pulled along the road
By horses harnessed to the front, **pulling** their heavy load.

How **cold** to sit up on the top beside the driver's seat,
I'd stay inside the carriage, where I could warm my feet.
I'd hear the horses whinny as they **galloped** on their way,
To get where we'd be going would take almost all day.

In the end we'd get there, and I would clamber down
Onto a street of **cobbles,** in an olden-days type town.
I'd see all the ladies, walking so sedately,
And saying to each other, *I hope you've been well lately.*

My Pen-Pal

I'm writing to my pen-pal
Who lives **miles** away from me,
Over the highest mountains
And beyond the deep blue sea.

I'll tell her all about the things
I did at school today,
And ask her all about herself –
What **games** she likes to play.

Does she play with dollies?
Or would she rather be
Outside in the garden
Where she can **climb** a tree?

She'll tell me all about herself –
Her age and her name,
And I bet we will discover
That we're pretty much the **same!**

One Man Went to Mow

One man went to mow,
Went to mow a meadow,
One man, and his dog,
Went to mow a meadow.
Two men went to mow,
Went to mow a meadow,
Two men, one man, and his dog,
Went to mow a meadow.
Three men went to mow,

Went to mow a meadow,
Three men, two men,
one man, and his dog,
Went to mow a meadow.
Four men went to mow,
Went to mow a meadow,
Four men, three men, two men,
one man, and his dog,
Went to mow a meadow.

You can keep adding verses as far as you can count.

Rapunzel

Once, a man and his wife were expecting a baby. A witch lived next door and had a garden which was full of rapunzel plants. The woman had such a longing to eat the tasty leaves.

"I just must eat rapunzel leaves," said the wife.

So the man went into the witch's garden and picked the leaves to **satisfy** his wife's craving.

The man picked the leaves every day, but one day the witch caught him. "Why are you **stealing** my leaves?" she said.

"My wife is expecting a baby and she has such a craving for rapunzel leaves," replied the man.

"You can have my leaves," said the witch, "but you must give me your baby."

When the baby was born, the man gave the baby to the witch, who called her Rapunzel.

Rapunzel grew into a beautiful woman with long hair. The witch took Rapunzel to a tower that had one window, but no door.

The witch would come to the tower and call, *"Rapunzel, Rapunzel, let down your hair."*

Rapunzel would let down her long

hair, and the witch would climb up it.

One day, a prince came by and heard Rapunzel singing. He wanted to get into the tower, but when he saw there was no door he hid, waited and watched.

After a while, the prince saw the witch and heard her call to Rapunzel. He watched as the witch climbed up and, when the witch had gone, he called, *"Rapunzel, Rapunzel, let down your hair."*

The prince climbed up and, when he saw Rapunzel, he fell in love. The prince visited her every day.

But the witch soon found out and was very angry.

She cut off Rapunzel's hair and sent her far away.

When the prince next came to visit, the witch let down Rapunzel's cut-off hair and the prince climbed up. When he saw the witch, he let go and fell down into a thorny bush. Sharp thorns went into his eyes, and he could no longer see.

The blind prince walked and walked until one day, he heard Rapunzel singing, and the two were reunited.

When Rapunzel heard what had happened to the prince, she cried, and her tears fell into the prince's eyes, washing away the thorns. The prince could see again! The prince and Rapunzel were married, and they lived happily ever after.

Jack Be Nimble

Jack be nimble,
Jack be quick,
Jack jump over
The candlestick.

The Magic Sea Shell

Once upon a time, there was a fisherman's daughter named Marina. On the days when her father was out at sea, Marina would wait for him on the beach and search for pretty shells to add to her collection.

On one such day, a **storm** began to blow in. As the sea grew rougher, Marina began to worry about her father.

Marina waited and watched, but there was no sign of her father's little fishing boat. As she waited, she saw other boats come in. "Have you seen my father's boat?" Marina asked them, but nobody had.

Marina was beginning to **despair** when she noticed a beautiful pink shell on the sands, shimmering more **brightly** than any she had ever seen. She picked it up, put it to her ear and heard a tiny voice:

"Out beyond the bay, sticking up above the waves, a man clings to a rock, waiting to be saved."

Marina ran for help and a brave crew of men set off to find her father. They sailed out into the stormy sea and, sure enough, just as the shell had said, they found Marina's father **clinging** onto a rock for dear life.

Marina never heard the shell's voice again, but she kept the shell and gave it pride of place in her collection.

Bookworm

Bookworm is the nickname that my mother gave to me,
Because I'd rather read a book than watch things on TV.
I like to read a story when I'm **curled** up snug in bed,
I often put away my toys and read a book instead.

A good **adventure** story is the kind that I like best,
With knights in gleaming armour saving maidens in distress.
Or sometimes I will read a book about geography,
And learn about the big wide world with many things to see.

A book is like a best friend, to take along with me.
Whatever I am doing and wherever I may be,
I'll pick up my latest read and open up the pages,
And, if nobody **bothers** me, I'll sit and read for ages!

Whoops-a-Daisy!

Clumsy elf, it's not your fault
That your fingers fumble.
The other elves all laugh at you
When you start to bumble.
You're only trying to help out –
I wish that they could see,
That you always do your best
Whatever that may be!

Whoops-a-daisy! Clumsy elf!
You're sliding in the snow!
It's not your fault if you're no good,
At watching where you go.
You're trying to stay upright,
But the snow lies in great mounds,
You do your best to hold on tight,
But – CRASH! you hit the ground.

The Lion and the Unicorn

The lion and the unicorn were fighting for the crown;
The lion beat the unicorn all around the town.
Some gave them white bread,
and some gave them brown;
Some gave them plum cake,
and drummed them out of town.

Billy Booster

Billy, Billy Booster,
Had a little rooster,
The rooster died,
And Billy cried.
Poor Billy Booster.

I Had a Little Puppy

I had a little puppy,
His name was Tiny Tim.
I put him in the bathtub,
To see if he could swim.
He drank all the water,
He ate a bar of soap –
The next thing you know
He had a bubble in his throat!

As I Was Going to St Ives

As I was going to St Ives,
I met a man with seven wives.
Each wife had seven sacks;
Each sack had seven cats;
Each cat had seven kits.
Kits, cats, sacks and wives.
How many were going to St Ives?

Birds of a Feather

Birds of a feather flock together
And so will pigs and swine;
Rats and mice shall have their choice,
And so shall I have mine.

Hey Diddle Diddle

Hey diddle diddle, the cat and the fiddle,
The cow jumped over the moon.
The little dog laughed to see such fun
And the dish ran away with the spoon!

Neptune's Surprise!

It was King Neptune's birthday and the seabed was buzzing with excitement. The merfolk had decided to throw a surprise party for their king, and everyone was busy wrapping presents and thinking of **surprises** for him.

Mimi the oyster had made Neptune a lovely shiny pearl, and some of the mermaids had baked a cake. But there was one little mermaid who was feeling sad. Mya wanted to find a very special present, but she couldn't think of anything to give her king. She was sitting all by herself still wondering what to do, when Snapper the crab sidled up to her to see why she wasn't busy getting ready for the party.

"Oh dear," sighed poor Mya. "I can't think of anything to give King Neptune. All the best ideas have gone."

"Don't worry," said Snapper. "There must be something special that you can give him." The friendly crab clicked his claws while he tried to think – Clickety, click! But neither of them could come up with a new idea.

"What are you giving Neptune?" Mya asked Snapper.

"I'm playing him a tune on my keyboard," he replied. "Basher Octopus, Jazzy Blowfish and Rocker Seahorse are playing too."

"Oh, how wonderful," gasped Mya. "Neptune will love that!"

"The only problem is that none of us can sing," sighed Snapper, "and we really wanted to sing 'Happy Birthday!' to him."

Mya perked up when she heard this, and Snapper couldn't understand why.

"You'll just have to wait and see!" Mya told him mysteriously, when he asked.

The party started and Neptune sat happily on his throne enjoying the wonderful surprise. Snapper and his band played some great tunes and everybody danced merrily. After a while, Mya made her way towards the stage and climbed up to join the band. She whispered something in Snapper's ear and then walked to the front.

Mya's voice rang out as she sang 'Happy Birthday!' to Neptune. She had a beautiful voice and everyone clapped and cheered. Nobody cheered louder than Neptune, who declared Mya's song the best present of all!

Jelly on the Plate

Jelly on the plate,
Jelly on the plate,
Wibble wobble,
Wibble, wobble,
Jelly on the plate.

Sweeties in the jar,
Sweeties in the jar,
Shake them up,
Shake them up,
Sweeties in the jar.

Candles on the cake,
Candles on the cake,
Blow them out,
Blow them out,
Puff, puff, **Puff!**

Jack and Guy

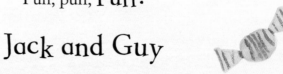

Jack and Guy went out in Rye,
And they found a little boy with one black eye.
Come, says Jack, let's knock him on the head.
No, says Guy, let's buy him some bread;
You buy one loaf and I'll buy two,
And we'll bring him up as other folk do.

I Scream

I scream, you scream,
We all scream for ice cream!

A Peanut

A peanut sat on the railway track,
His heart was all a-flutter;
Along came a train – the 9.15 –
Toot! Toot! Peanut butter!

Dibbity, Dibbity, Dibbity, Doe

Dibbity, dibbity, dibbity, doe,
Give me a pancake and I'll go.
Dibbity, dibbity, dibbity, ditter,
Please give me a lovely fritter.

Ten Green Bottles

Ten green bottles, standing on a wall,
Ten green bottles, standing on a wall,
And if one green bottle should accidentally fall,
There'd be nine green bottles, standing on a wall.

A Windy Day

On sunny days we play outside,
On rainy days we shelter.
On snowy days we we wear warm clothes
And when it's hot, we swelter!

Of all the weather that exists,
The kind that I like best,
Without a doubt are windy days,
South, north, east or west.

Any way the wind can blow
Will be just fine for me,
Because my favourite thing to do
Is flying kites, you see.

So blow wind, blow – I will not mind
If you howl day and night.
While others hold onto their hats,
I'll be flying kites!

The Big, Red Train!

Peep! Peep! The whistle's blowing,
The bright green light is glowing,
The big, red train is going,
Toot! Toot! We're on our way!

Chug! Chug! The wheels are turning,
The red hot coal is burning,
And now my heart is churning,
Let's ride along all day!

But soon we're at the station,
It's time to put the brakes on,
We've reached our destination.
Hip! Hip! Hip! Hooray!

The Emperor's New Clothes

Once upon a time there was a foolish emperor who loved clothes. One day two tailors came to town. They knew the emperor was foolish, and they wanted to trick him.

"We have some special cloth," they said. "It is so special that only very clever people can see it. Foolish people cannot! See how beautiful it is?"

The tailors did not really have any cloth, so the emperor could not see anything. But he did not want to look foolish. "It's very beautful," he said.

"The cloth will make wonderful clothes," said the tailors.

So the king ordered the tailors to make a new suit for him.

"Certainly, your majesty," said the tailors. "That will cost one hundred gold coins." So the emperor gave them the gold. "Come and see the clothes next week," said the tailors.

The next week, the emperor went to see the clothes. "Look!" said the tailors. "Isn't it fabulous?" But of course the emperor could still see nothing at all. But, not wanting to reveal himself as a fool, he said, **"Gorgeous!"**

"Your suit will be ready next week," the tailors told the emperor, ushering him out of the door.

The next week, the tailors went to see the emperor. "You will look **sensational** in your new clothes," they said. Still the emperor saw nothing but, wanting to appear clever, he allowed the tailors to dress him in his new suit.

The emperor went into town. "Look at my new clothes," he said to his subjects. "They are the best in the world, but foolish people will not be able to see them." Nobody could see the clothes, but they did not want to look foolish. "Look at the emperor's **wonderful** new clothes," they said.

A boy and a girl saw the emperor.

"Look! The emperor has no clothes on," they said and started laughing. Soon everyone was laughing at the emperor.

By this time, the two tailors were long gone – one hundred gold coins richer than they were before!

The Boy Next Door

Abigail had known the boy next door for as long as she could remember. His name was Andrew and they had played together when they were little. But now they liked different things from each other. Andrew often teased Abigail when she played with her dolls or had her friends round for a sleepover.

One day, Abigail was walking home from school when she heard Andrew riding up behind her on his bike.

"Hey, carrot-top!" he called to her. "Are you entering the poetry competition tomorrow?"

Abigail hated to be teased about her auburn hair, and **blushed** scarlet. She turned into her garden gate and hurried up the path to her door without replying.

Abigail was going to enter the poetry competition. She had written a **wonderful** poem about her pet cat to read out.

That night, Abigail's mother gave her a long, yellow dress to wear for the competition.

"I wore this dress when I was your age," explained Abigail's mother. "It brought me luck when I entered a competition and I thought it might do the same for you."

Abigail sighed. It was a lovely

dress, but she was worried that Andrew would **tease** her about it.

The next day, Abigail was nervous about the competition all day. When the time came for the competition to begin, Abigail changed into her yellow dress and went backstage to wait for her turn.

Then Abigail spotted Andrew. She tried to **hide** behind a curtain but Andrew spotted her and came over.

This time he was the one to blush. "H-h-hello, Abigail," he stammered. "G-gosh! You look lovely in your dress." Andrew realised that Abigail was turning into a pretty young lady and that he didn't want to tease her at all.

The two neighbours shook hands, wished each other luck and waited **nervously** for their turns. When the time came, each of them read their poems well and received loud applause. When the winners were to be announced, Abigail and Andrew stood next to each other waiting for the result.

"We have joint winners for this competition," announced the head teacher. "Abigail and Andrew share first place. They were both so good that the judges couldn't choose between them!" Andrew and Abigail were so pleased, not just about winning – they had discovered that they still had something in common. Now they could be friends again!

The Best of Friends

Cleo the horse and Daphne Duck were the best of friends. They never ever argued... well, **hardly** ever!

One rainy day when the friends were stuck indoors, Daphne and Cleo were feeling bored.

"I've got a good idea, let's play with building blocks," quacked Daphne.

"Neigh! I've got a better idea – why don't we put on a show?" whinnied Cleo. "I could do my special tap-dance and you could tell some of your funny jokes!"

"That's a good idea, but I'd really prefer to play with the building blocks right now," replied Daphne.

"Show!" shouted Cleo.

"Blocks!" shouted back Daphne.

The two best friends just couldn't agree what to do.

"Well, I'm playing with the building blocks," snapped Daphne. "I can quite easily play by myself!" And she set to work building a lovely tower from the blocks.

"Neigh! Suit yourself," said Cleo, and she started galloping around the room practising her tap-dancing. "I'll put on my own show, so there!"

Daphne was just finishing her beautiful tower made from the blocks when, all of a sudden, Cleo came tippety-tapping across the room – **crash!**

Cleo fell right on top of Daphne's tower and landed in a heap of blocks. Daphne was furious.

"I'm sorry," said Cleo rubbing her nose where a block had landed on it. "I'll help you to re-build it." Daphne was still feeling rather cross, but agreed to let Cleo help. The two friends set to work.

"Why don't we build something different this time?" suggested Daphne.

"What would you like to build?" asked Cleo.

"Well... er... how about a lovely stage?" said Daphne. "Then we could put on that show you were talking about."

The two friends set to work. Soon they had built a lovely stage. It didn't really matter that there was no audience. Cleo and Daphne put on a wonderful show. Cleo's tap-dance was followed by Daphne's comedy act.

"What time does a duck wake up?" joked Daphne. "At the quack of dawn!"

Cleo laughed so much that she made the stage **fall** down. But it didn't matter, they'd soon think of another game to play together!

Jingle's Bell!

Jingle was Lottie's best toy of all. He wasn't exactly a bear and he wasn't quite a bunny. He had a **bell** in one ear, which was how he'd got his name.

One day, Lottie woke up to find it had snowed overnight. She was very excited and grabbed Jingle by the paw to take him with her for a closer look.

All Lottie's friends were out, and ready for some fun. The games went on all morning, until Lottie was called in for lunch by her mother.

"See you later," she called. And she looked around for Jingle. Soft white mounds of snow had covered everything and, although she looked everywhere, she couldn't find him.

"Don't worry," said Lottie's mum. "We know he's out there somewhere, we're sure to find him later." But although everyone searched through the afternoon, there was simply too much snow and Jingle remained lost.

It was nearly **bedtime** and Lottie was getting really worried.

"How will I be able to sleep without Jingle?" she sighed,

staring out of the window still hoping to spot her soft friend. As she sat there she noticed a little bird pecking at the snow.

"Poor little thing," said Lottie's mum. "I expect he's

looking for something to eat."

As the bird continued to peck the ground, Lottie heard a strange sound. It was a kind of **muffled** tinkle. Had she imagined it? No, there it it was again!

"Can you hear that sound?" Lottie asked, but her mum couldn't hear anything.

Suddenly, Lottie **jumped** up off her chair. She had just realised what the sound could be. She rushed out into her garden, not even stopping to put on her coat and wellies.

"Hey! Where are you rushing off to?" called Lottie's mum.

Lottie ran over to where the little bird had been pecking and dug with her bare hands, hoping her hunch was right.

Yes, there he was! She could see his little ear **poking** up through the snow, and she kept on digging until she could pull out her cold, soggy friend.

Lottie had got nearly as cold and wet as Jingle, and they both sat by the fire to warm up. Lottie sipped at her hot chocolate drink.

"I told you he'd show up," smiled Lottie's mum.

"He was **saved** by his bell!" laughed Lottie.

And that night, she gave her friend such a big hug that it nearly squeezed his stuffing out!

Wish Upon a Star

If there was one thing that James wanted more than anything else, it was a new friend. He had just moved to a new area and, although he liked his new house, he **missed** his old friends.

"You'll make some new friends soon enough," his mother told him. But for now, James only had his cat, Pumpkin, for company.

James was building a den in the garden. He had found the perfect spot for it and had made some walls from tree branches. It was fun, but James thought it would be even better fun if he had a **friend** to help him.

One night when the sky was clear, James noticed the most beautiful star shining **brightly** in the sky. James thought that it might be a lucky star, so he made a wish.

"Oh, beautiful star, I wish I could make a new friend," he called up into the night.

The next day, James went

out to play in his garden. He was busy
working on his new den when he heard
a strange noise – thwack! James
looked around, but couldn't see what
was making the strange sound.
Thwack! There it was again.
Then, James felt Pumpkin
rubbing his furry body against
his leg and he bent down to give him a
stroke. Pumpkin meowed loudly and
ran off.

"Hey, Pumpkin!" called James. "Where are you off to?"
He followed his cat, who jumped up onto the garden wall
and began to meow even more loudly. He reached up to lift
Pumpkin down again, and it was then that he found out where
the strange sound had been coming from. Thwack!

As James peeped into the next-door garden, he noticed a
boy batting a ball against the wall.

"Hello," said James. "What are you playing?"

"I'm playing tennis, but it's not much fun on my own,"
replied the boy.

The boy, who was called Ben, asked James if he'd like to
play. James was so happy – his wish had come true! They
played ball all morning and then, after lunch, they set to work
finishing off James's den.

That night, James looked up at the night sky. "Thank you,
star," James whispered into the night... "wherever you are!"

Flying High

Flying high, swooping low,
Loop-the-loop and round they go.
Catching currents, soaring fast,
Feathered friends come sweeping past.

Feathers

Cackle, cackle, Mother Goose,
Have you any feathers loose?
Truly have I, pretty fellow,
Half enough to fill a pillow.
Here are quills, take one or two,
And down to make a bed for you.

Cut Thistles

Cut thistles in May,
They'll grow in a day;
Cut them in June,
That is too soon;
Cut them in July,
Then they will die.

Sparrow

Little brown sparrow, sat upon a tree,
Way up in the branches, safe as he can be!
Hopping through the green leaves, he will play,
High above the ground is where he will stay.

Little Ginger Cat

Little ginger cat,
Sitting in the sun,
Watching all the birds
Flying just for fun.
Hear them chirp and tweet,
As they fly so free,
Just as if to say,
"You cannot catch me!"

Run, Little Mice

Run, little mice, little mice run!
Don't let that naughty cat have his fun.
Hide beneath the floor, until he's gone away,
And then, little mice, come on out and play!

Bedtime with Gran

When I snuggle up at night,
There's no one that I'd rather
Tuck me in all nice and tight
Than my dear grandmother.

"Which story would you like to read?"
My sweet old gran will say.
I always pick the longest one
To make sure that she stays.

She takes me to another world
Of fairies, queens and kings.
And when she kisses me goodnight,
I dream wonderful things.

A Snowy Day

On this chilly winter's day,
My breath hangs in the air,
Frozen in this snowy scene,
I watch it linger there.

A glistening carpet covers all,
Turning the green grass white,
And crunches with each footstep,
A wintery delight!

First I'll make snow angels,
And then a snowman, too.
And last of all, you guessed it—
A snowball-fight with you!

Ugly Troll

Under the bridge and down by the stream,
Lives a **big** creature who'll make you scream!
His fearsome face and **bellowing** howl
Are quite repulsive – utterly **foul**!

Ugly Troll! You're a fright to my eyes!
Ugly Troll! You're an **enormous** size!
Ugly Troll! You're as gross as can be,
But Ugly Troll – **you don't scare me**!

Didn't his mother teach him to wash?
When I stand near him – the **smell**... oh my, gosh!
He can threaten to eat me, roar and yell,
But the **scariest** thing about him is his smell!

Magic Seed

I found a tiny little seed
And planted it outside.
Almost at once it started
To **grow** up, tall and wide.

It sprouted leaves from everywhere,
And soon became quite big.
I'm not sure what it is yet —
Apples, peas or figs?

No matter how it turns out,
I know that it will be
My own completely special
Something-or-other tree!

The Special Rose

Princess Jasmine was never happier than when she was in her flower meadow. As she walked through the scented field, she would admire the bright colours and pretty petals of the poppies, cornflowers and wild orchids that grew there. "The world is such a beautiful place," she thought to herself.

One day, Princess Jasmine noticed a **perfect** red rose growing amongst the wild flowers. As it did not belong where it was growing, she picked the special rose and placed it by her bed so that she could admire its velvety petals as she drifted off to sleep.

Princess Jasmine usually slept soundly, but that night she dreamt she walked beyond her pretty flower meadow and

down a path that she had never seen before. At the end of it was a tiny cottage where an old woman sat **weeping** her heart out.

The next morning, Princess Jasmine set off for her flower meadow and, when she got there, she looked for the little path. At first she found no trace of it at all, but then she noticed another red rose, just like the one she had picked the day before. She picked this rose too and, as she plucked it from the ground, a path opened up before her very eyes.

Princess Jasmine picked her way carefully along the path and found that, just has she had dreamt, the path led to a little cottage. The door was slightly open and she heard the sound of someone crying from within. Princess Jasmine tiptoed in and found the old woman, weeping.

"Why are you crying so?" asked the princess.

"I am sad because I am all alone," replied the woman. She explained that she loved to grow red roses, but now she was too old to tend them and so they had all died.

"What is the world without beauty?" the old woman asked Princess Jasmine.

"I have the most beautiful flower meadow, just up the path from here," the kind princess told the old woman. "You can visit it any time you like. I go there every day and so you will not be lonely any more."

From then on, the old woman met princess Jasmine every day, and they admired the wild meadow flowers together. Although Princess Jasmine kept on looking, she never found another special red rose growing there.

A Swishy Fishy Day!

Madison and Ethan were the best of friends. They swam everywhere together and loved to play with the friendly fish.

"Let's go for a chariot ride," said Ethan one day. The water was **calm** and clear, so Madison agreed. Liam the seahorse pulled them along in a shell for a chariot, and the two friends rode around the seabed followed by some friendly fish.

"**Whee!**" squealed Ethan.

"**Go faster!**" called Madison. Liam swam just as fast as he could, pulling the two excited friends along behind him. But he swam so fast that the little fish couldn't keep up.

"**Wait for us,**" they called, but Liam sped on and on.

When Liam finally stopped, Ethan and Madison clambered out of the chariot to explore.

But after a while, the sea began to grow rougher and the

water became cloudy. Madison and Ethan climbed back into the chariot and Liam set off for home.

But, oh dear! Where was home? Liam had been swimming so fast he couldn't remember which way they had come, and now the water was so murky he couldn't see which way to go.

"We're lost," cried Madison. "How will we get home?"

"Don't worry," said Ethan, trying his best to comfort his friend. But he was worried too.

They came to a big rock that Ethan thought he recognised, but Madison wasn't so sure.

"It's no good," she sobbed. "We were going so fast I can't remember which rocks we passed on the way."

Just then, some little bubbles floated out of a hole in the rock, and out swam their little fishy friends.

"There you are!" said the smallest red fish. "We couldn't keep up with you so we stopped to take a rest in this rock."

"Do you know the way back?" asked Liam.

"Yes, follow us!" called the fish as they swam home.

When Ethan and Madison got home, they thanked the fish and gave Liam a big hug.

"Next time we go out," said Liam, "let's pay more attention to where we are."

Ethan and Madison happily agreed. They hadn't liked being lost one bit!

The Enormous Turnip

Once upon a time there was an old man who loved to grow vegetables. The old man had some turnip seeds, which he planted in his garden.

Every day the old man watered his seeds. All the turnips began to grow. But one turnip began to grow more than the others. The turnip got bigger and bigger and **bigger** still!

Every day the turnip grew some more. Soon it was the biggest turnip he had ever seen. The old man was very excited.

"Look at my **enormous** turnip," he said to his wife. "I can't wait to eat it!"

One day the old man said, "Today's the day! It's time to pull up my enormous turnip." So the old man pulled as hard as he could. But he **couldn't** pull up the enormous turnip. So the old man called to his wife, "Can you help me pull up my enormous turnip?" So the old woman pulled the old man.

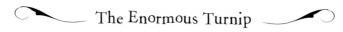

They pulled as hard as they could, but the enormous turnip wouldn't even budge.

So the old man said to a boy, "Can you help me pull up my enormous turnip?"

So the boy pulled the old woman and the old woman pulled the old man. They all pulled and pulled, but they couldn't pull up the enormous turnip.

So the old man said to a girl, "Can you help me pull up my enormous turnip? So the girl pulled the boy, the boy pulled the old woman and the old woman pulled the old man.

But they couldn't pull up the enormous turnip. So the old man said to his donkey and his goat, "Can you help me pull up my enormous turnip?" So the donkey and the goat pulled the girl who pulled the boy who pulled the old woman who pulled the old man. They pulled and they pulled and they pulled and… out came the enormous turnip with a pop!

The old man was very happy. "Look at my enormous turnip," he said. "Now we can eat turnip for tea."

So the goat and the donkey and the girl and the boy and the old woman and the old man all had turnip for tea.

And it was the most delicious turnip that any of them had ever tasted!

Can I See Across the Hills?

Can I see across the hills,
And over to the sea?
Can I see over the sea,
To where more land may be?

Little Bird

Little bird, little bird,
Where do you live?
Up in yonder wood, sir,
On a hazel twig.

Old Farmer Giles

Old Farmer Giles,
He went seven miles
With his faithful dog Old Rover;
And his faithful dog Old Rover,
When he came to the stiles,
Took a run, and jumped clean over.

Red Stockings

Red stockings, blue stockings,
Shoes tied up with silver;
A red rosette upon my breast
And a gold ring on my finger.

Fidget

As little Jenny Wren
Was sitting by the shed,
She waggled with her tail,
She nodded with her head;
She waggled with her tail,
She nodded with her head;
As little Jenny Wren
Was sitting by the shed.

Little Dove

Little dove, little dove, sitting in a tree,
Wondering where her friends could be.
"Have you seen them, little wren?"
"I've seen them fly by, now and then."

Favourite Things

I've written down a list
Of all my favourite things;
Rainbows and fairy cakes
And butterfly wings.

A journey on a train,
A visit from a friend,
Candyfloss and ice cream –
The list might never end!

Each time I think of one,
I add it to the rest,
It's fun to keep a track
Of things that I like best.

I roll it in a scroll,
And keep it safe from harm,
My list of favourite things
Is longer than my arm!

My Grandpa's Trunk

A wooden chest stands on the floor,
Just inside my grandpa's door.
What hidden secrets does it hold?
Perhaps he has some pirate's gold!

Grandpa, I ask, please may I see
What's inside? He looks at me
With his kind old twinkling eyes,
And says I'm in for a surprise!

He carefully opens up the trunk,
I hear the big old lock go Clunk!
The lid is open, eagerly
I look inside and what I see...

Is Grandpa's treasure! Nothing gold,
No sparkling diamonds to behold,
But lots of books and this and that,
Worn-out clothes, and an old straw hat.

Serena's Lucky Find

Serena the mermaid was sitting on a rock one day, combing her long dark hair, when her friend Sheldon the turtle popped his head out of the water.

"Please will you come for a swim with me, Serena?" asked Sheldon. "The water is so calm and clear today, there will be lots of lovely things to see." So Serena slipped down off the rock and into the water with a **splash!**

As the two friends swam along, they saw beautiful coral and colourful seaweed, gently swaying in the soft current.

"You're right, Sheldon," said Serena happily, "there are lots of lovely things to see today."

As they swam along further, they met Mrs Clownfish. She looked very worried.

"I've lost my four little babies," she sobbed. "Please help me find them."

Serena and Sheldon swam off to search for the baby fish.

"Don't worry," they called behind them. "We'll soon find them in this lovely clear water." As Serena and Sheldon swam on, they saw something glinting brightly in the water ahead.

"I wonder what that can be?" said Serena, swimming towards the shimmering water ahead. **"It's treasure!"** she called out to Sheldon, who was paddling as fast as he could to catch up with her.

Sheldon and Serena gasped in amazement at all the beautiful treasure that was spilling out of an old wooden chest. There were rubies, pearls and many other colourful jewels. The two friends picked up pieces of treasure to admire them, and to try on the lovely pieces of jewellery. Then Serena heard a strange sound coming from the treasure chest. Tap! Tap! Tap! It seemed to be coming from inside a large golden locket.

Feeling a little bit nervous, Serena carefully prised open the locket – and out swam the four little baby fish!

"There you are!" exclaimed Serena. "Your mummy has been worried about you!" The little fish swam back behind Sheldon and Serena.

Mrs Clownfish was so happy to see her babies.

"We had a lucky find!" laughed Serena.

"Come here, my little treasures," said Mrs Clownfish, as she gave each of her little fish a lovely hug.

Sleep, Baby, Sleep

Sleep, baby, sleep,
Your father tends the sheep.
Your mother shakes the dreamland tree
And from it fall sweet dreams for thee.
Sleep, baby, sleep.

Sleep, baby, sleep.
Our cottage vale is deep.
The little lamb is on the green,
With snowy fleece, so soft and clean.
Sleep, baby, sleep.

Hush-a-Bye, Baby

Hush-a-bye, baby, on the treetop,
When the wind blows, the cradle will rock;
When the bough breaks, the cradle will fall,
Down will come baby, cradle and all.

Crescent Moon

Crescent moon, please shine your light
On this clear and starry night.
Although I see just part of you,
I know you'll stay the whole night through.

O Lady Moon

O Lady Moon, your horns point towards the east:
Shine, be increased.
O Lady Moon, your horns point towards the west:
Wane, be at rest.

Ding, Dong, Bell

Ding, dong, bell,
Pussycat's in the well!
Who put her in?
Little Tommy Green.
Who pulled her out?
Little Johnny Stout.
What a naughty boy was that
To try to drown poor pussycat,
Who never did any harm,
But killed the mice in his father's barn.

Muffin Man

Have you seen the muffin man,
The muffin man, the muffin man,
Have you seen the muffin man
That lives in Drury Lane?
Yes I've seen the muffin man,
That lives in Drury lane!

Grinding Corn

Early in the misty morn
The miller's up to grind some corn.
Wheels turn, sacks will fill,
As he grinds corn in his mill.

The Miller of Dee

There was a jolly miller
Lived on the river Dee:
He worked and sang from morn till night,
No lark so blithe as he;
And this the burden of his song for ever used to be:
I jump me jerrime jee!
I care for nobody – no! not I,
Since nobody cares for me.

The Longest Night

Once upon a time, there lived a wicked witch who made the sun disappear. The people of the land grew poor, as there was no sunshine to grow the crops. Nobody knew whether it was night or day, but they carried on their lives as best they could.

One day, a traveller was passing through the land and he decided to rest for the night at an inn.

"I will just stay for one night, and I'll be on my way again in the morning," he told the inn-keeper.

But when the traveller woke up, he found it was still night time. "How strange," he thought to himself. "I feel wide awake and yet it is still dark outside."

The traveller went downstairs and was amazed to see everyone up and about. The inn-keeper explained to the traveller about the wicked witch's spell.

"But this is terrible!" exclaimed the traveller. "How can you live without sunshine?" The traveller decided to trick

the wicked witch, and he came up with a plan. He went to the witch's house and he started to dig a hole. When he had finished one hole, he dug another and then another. Soon the witch came out to see what he was doing.

"What are you doing here?" asked the angry witch.

"I am digging for my lost treasure," replied the cunning traveller. "Many years ago, I buried it here, but now I can't find it because it is too dark to see properly."

The witch loved treasure. "Ha, ha!" she cackled to herself. "I will steal the treasure from this fool when he finds it." And she reversed her spell.

As the sun came up for the first time in many years, tiny green shoots began to push up to the surface from below the ground. Before long there was one perfect golden flower.

"Here is my treasure!" exclaimed the traveller, pointing to the flower. The witch was furious – she had been tricked! The land became sunny again and everyone (except the wicked witch) lived happily ever after.

Thank You for Being my Friend

It was a dark night. In the bedroom, nothing stirred. Nothing except a heap of bright wrapping paper on the end of the bed. The paper **rustled**. It **crackled**. It **shook**.

And then out popped a toy horse.

"Hello!" said the horse. "I'm Cleo."

But there was no answer, so Cleo trotted across the bed to see who she could find.

"I can't be the only toy in this bedroom," she thought. "I hope I find somebody soon. I don't like the dark."

Cleo looked around her and saw some strange shapes in the dark room. She felt lonely and frightened. "I'm scared," she shivered. "Those shapes look like monsters to me!" Cleo thought she saw a thin monster… a plump monster… a tall monster… and a monster with no head!

Then Cleo saw a faint gleam of light and she tiptoed carefully towards the door to see where it was coming from.

"Oh, it's only the moon," said Cleo. Suddenly, a cloud slid over the moon and everything went dark. And then something downstairs went **Bong! Bong! Bong!**

Cleo nearly jumped out of her skin. "It's a monster, coming to get me!" she whinnied. "Help!"

Cleo spun on her hooves and galloped back the way she had come. As she hurtled into the bedroom, she tripped over and landed on top of something that was lying on the floor.

"Ugh," groaned the Thing drowsily.

"Who... who are you?"

"I'm C-Cleo," muttered Cleo, feeling very frightened. "P-please don't **gobble** me up!"

Then the moon came out again and Cleo saw that the Thing was a fluffy yellow duck.

"I'm Daphne," smiled the duck. "And why would I want to gobble you up?"

Cleo told Daphne all about the monsters.

"I won't let any monsters get you," said Daphne.

"Promise?" asked Cleo with a big **yawn.**

"Promise," said Daphne kindly. "Why don't you snuggle down with me?"

"You won't leave me, will you?" said Cleo.

"No. You're safe now. Night-night," said Daphne.

"Night-night," said Cleo.

The next morning, Cleo peeped out from under Daphne's

wing. She blinked in the bright sunlight.

"Morning sleepyhead," quacked Daphne. "Come and meet all those monsters you thought you saw last night!" Cleo shot back under Daphne's wing.

"Don't worry," laughed Daphne. "They weren't real monsters – it was just your imagination!"

Cleo found out that the thin monster was… a lamp! The plump monster was… a heap of cushions! The tall monster was… a wardrobe! The headless monster was… a dressing gown! And the terrible monster, the one that Cleo thought was chasing her, turned out to be… the grandfather clock!

Tick, tock, tick tock!

"I've been really silly," smiled Cleo.

"No, you've not," said Daphne. "Lots of things look scary in the dark when you can't see what they really are."

"Now I've got you as a friend, I don't think I'll be scared any more," said Cleo. And she was quite right. After that she was never scared of the dark again.

The Butterfly Ball

Felicia was a dressmaker. Her dresses were so beautiful that the Fairy Queen herself had asked Felicia to make her a special gown for the Butterfly Ball. Every year in Fairyland, the queen threw a special party in honour of their friends the butterflies.

"I would like a really special dress this year," the queen told Felicia. "It needs to be something totally different from anything there has been before."

Felicia tried her best to design something special, but, although all her ideas were pretty, she had not come up with anything really new. Now it was the day of the ball, and Felicia was very worried.

As Felicia was wondering what she could do, she heard a tiny little cry and she noticed a pretty little butterfly stuck in a spider's web. Felicia very carefully set her free.

"Oh, thank you," said the butterfly. "I thought I would be stuck here forever, and I didn't want to miss the Butterfly Ball tonight." When the little butterfly mentioned the ball, she noticed that Felicia started looking rather sad.

"What's the matter?" asked the butterfly.

"I am supposed to be making a very special dress for the Fairy Queen," explained Felicia, "but I haven't come up with a new idea for her yet, and now time is running out."

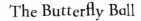

"We butterflies think that flowers are the prettiest things ever," said the butterfly. "If I wanted to look extra-special, I would dress up as a flower."

That gave Felicia the most wonderful idea.

"I know just what I can make for the queen," she told the butterfly, "but I'll need your help to gather as many flower petals as you can find."

The butterfly happily agreed. "My friends will help too," she said, as she fluttered away.

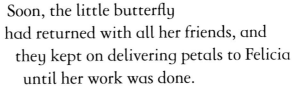

Soon, the little butterfly had returned with all her friends, and they kept on delivering petals to Felicia until her work was done.

That night, the Fairy Queen looked very special indeed. She wore a beautiful dress made from the softest, scented flower petals. The butterflies all thought that the Fairy Queen looked more beautiful than ever.

"Thank you, Felicia!" beamed the Fairy Queen. "This certainly is a very special dress."

Goldy Locks, Goldy Locks

Goldy Locks, Goldy Locks,
Wilt thou be mine?
Thou shall not wash dishes,
Nor yet feed the swine;
But sit on a cushion,
And sew a fine seam,
And feed upon strawberries,
Sugar and cream.

Gilly Silly Jarter

Gilly Silly Jarter,
Who has lost a garter
In a shower of rain.
The miller found it,
And the miller gave it
To Silly again.

Anna Maria

Anna Maria she sat on the fire;
The fire was too hot, she sat on the pot;
The pot was too round, she sat on the ground;
The ground was too flat, she sat on the cat;
The cat ran away with Maria on her back.

Mr Punchinello

Oh! Mother, I shall be married
To Mr Punchinello.
To Mr Punch,
To Mr Joe,
To Mr Nell,
To Mr Lo,
Mr Punch, Mr Joe,
Mr Nell, Mr Lo,
To Mr Punchinello.

I Am a Pretty Little Dutch Girl

I am a pretty little Dutch girl,
As pretty as can be.
And all the boys in the neighbourhood
Are crazy over me!

A Pretty Little Girl

A pretty little girl in a round-eared cap
I met in the street the other day;
She gave me such a thump,
That my heart it went bump;
I thought I should have fainted away!

Fields of Gold

When the summer's over
And the sun is losing heat,
The rolling fields around me
Are full with ripened wheat.

A glowing golden carpet
Gently swaying as it stands,
Waiting for the farmer
To harvest from his land.

When the grains are gathered
And the straw lies on the ground,
We'll bale it and then stack it
Into lovely golden mounds.

Sleepyheads

Where do you go to, sleepyheads,
When you're fast asleep?
We drift away in a silver shell
In our slumber, deep.

What do you dream of, Sleepyheads,
In your beautiful silver shell?
We dream of grassy meadows
And a magic wishing-well.

What do you hope for, sleepyheads,
When you make your wishes?
We wish to see a mermaid
And some flying fishes.

Humpty Dumpty

Humpty Dumpty
Sat on a wall.
Humpty Dumpty
Had a great fall;
All the king's horses
And all the king's men
Couldn't put Humpty together again!

Twinkle, Twinkle, Little Star

Twinkle, twinkle, little star,
How I wonder what you are!
Up above the world so high,
Like a diamond in the sky.

When the blazing sun is gone,
When he nothing shines upon,
Then you show your little light,
Twinkle, twinkle all the night.

In the dark blue sky you keep,
And often through your
curtains peep,
For you never shut your eye,
Till the sun is in the sky.

As your bright and tiny spark,
Lights the traveller in the dark –
Though I know not what you are,
Twinkle, twinkle, little star.

The Princess and the Pea

Once upon a time there was a lonely prince.

"You should find yourself a princess to marry," said his mother, the queen. But the prince didn't want to marry just anyone.

"I will only marry a **real** princess," he said. The prince had met many beautiful girls. They wore golden crowns and fine jewels, but they were not real princesses.

That night, during a thunderstorm, there was a knock at the door. The prince opened the door and there stood a girl.

"I am a princess," she said.

The prince liked the girl, but wanted to be sure that she was a real princess.

"I will find out if this girl is a real princess or not," said the queen. The queen got a hard dried pea, and she made a bed for the princess that was twenty mattresses and twenty quilts high.

"This is your bed," the queen said to the princess. The princess had never seen such a high bed before, but she climbed up into it.

"Good night," said the princess. She tried to snuggle down

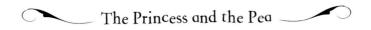

and go to sleep, but she felt very uncomfortable and was awake all night.

"**Did you sleep well?**" asked the queen the next morning.

"No, I was awake all night," said the princess. "There was something hard in the bed."

"Only a real princess could feel a pea under so many mattresses," said the queen.

The prince and the real princess were married, and they lived happily ever after.

Benji's New Friends

Benji the bear sat on the end of the bed, feeling a little bit lonely. He was new here and he hadn't seen anyone else in the bedroom.

He watched a moonbeam slip through a gap in the curtains and slide across the bed.

"I wish that I had someone to play with," he whispered.

"Did I hear someone say they wanted to play?" asked a voice. The lid of the toy box flew open, and out climbed a dangly legged, spotty horse.

"Hi, I'm Cleo… and I love to play!"

Boing! Boing!

Cleo jumped onto the bed and began to bounce up and down.

"Where did you come from?" she asked.

"From the birthday party," replied Benji. "I was a present."

"Did someone mention a party?" A friendly looking monkey poked his head around the curtain. "Why weren't Rosie and I invited?"

A floppy-eared rabbit appeared beside him.

"Max and I love parties!" Rosie the rabbit told Benji. "And so does Humph."

"Who's Humph?" asked Benji.

A loud yawn came from inside a box. Then a bright-blue hippo slowly lifted his head.

"I am!" he said. "A party…" he continued thoughtfully. "That means food. And I'm hungry! Is there anything left to eat?"

"I think there are some cakes in the kitchen," replied Benji, "but do you think we should…?"

But Humph was already through the door!

"Oh!" said Benji, looking at the other toys. "Should we go after him?"

Benji was bumping down the stairs after Humph when Cleo zoomed past.

"This is fun!" she neighed.

"Wait for me!" called Benji.

In the kitchen, Humph was about to take a bite out of a leftover cupcake with a candle in it.

The candle was already halfway into Humph's mouth. Benji grabbed it just in time.

"Excuse me," he explained, "but you aren't meant to eat that bit."

"Thanks, Benji. You're smart. I wish I knew things like that," grumbled Humph.

Before Benji could explain about the candle, he heard Rosie yell loudly. Benji raced back up to the bedroom where he found Rosie hiding under the bed. She had seen a big owl swoop past the window and it had given her quite a fright.

"Don't worry," said Benji, and he explained to everyone that owls never came inside people's houses and that they were all quite safe.

"Benji, will you always be here to look after us?" Cleo asked him. Benji gave a tiny little smile. It was nice to feel wanted. "Of course," he replied.

Humph was tired from their adventure. "How am I going to sleep when I'm so hungry?" he sniffed, settling back down on the bed.

Cleo and Rosie giggled. They danced around on the bed. Max joined in.

"Why don't we all play in the garden tomorrow?" Rosie suggested.

"What's your garden like?" asked Benji.

"I'll show you," said Cleo, and she helped Benji up to have a look out of the window.

"Wow!" he said. "It looks really exciting. Are you going to play in the garden, Humph?"

"Humph!" said Humph sleepily. "It's such a long way to the garden. I might just have a little nap instead."

Benji smiled at his new sleepy friend.

Cleo jumped back onto the bed and started to bounce. Benji looked up at the moon. He had a feeling that he wouldn't be lonely any more.

"I wish that tomorrow will be as much fun as today," he whispered.

Then Benji turned to his new friends, took a huge leap, and began to bounce on the bed.

"Here's to friends!" he laughed.

Birds on a Stone

There were two birds sat on a stone,
Fa, la, la, la, lal, de;
One flew away, then there was one,
Fa, la, la, la, lal, de;
The other flew after, and then there were none,
Fa, la, la, la, lal de;
And so the poor stone was left all alone,
Fa, la, la, la, lal, de!

There Was an Old Crow

There was an old crow
Sat upon a clod:
There's an end of my song,
That's odd!

On Oath

As I went to Bonner,
I met a pig without a wig,
Upon my word and honour.

Red Sky at Night

Red sky at night; shepherd's delight.
Red sky in the morning; shepherd's warning.

Greedy Tom

Jimmy the Mowdy
Made a great crowdy;
Barney O'Neal
Found the meal;
Old Jack Rutter
Sent two stone of butter;
The Laird of the Hot
Boiled it in his pot;
And Big Tom of the Hall
He supped it all.

The Ostrich

Here is the ostrich straight and tall,
Nodding his head above us all.
Here is the spider scuttling around,
Treading so lightly on the ground.
Here are the birds that fly so high,
Spreading their wings across the sky.
Here are the children fast asleep,
And in the night the owls do peep,
"Tuit tuwhoo, tuit tuwhoo!"

Chicken Licken

One day, Chicken Licken was in the woods when, BOINK! an acorn fell onto her head.

"Ruffle my feathers!" said Chicken Licken. "The sky is falling down. I must tell the king at once." And off she ran.

On her way, Chicken Licken met Cocky Locky who was on her way to the woods.

"Oh, don't go!" clucked Chicken Licken. "I was there a moment ago, and the sky fell on my head! I'm off to tell the king right away, you can come with me." And off they hurried.

Soon they met Ducky Lucky on his way for a swim in the pond.

"Oh, stop, Ducky Lucky!" squawked Chicken Licken. "The sky in the woods is falling down! We're off to tell the king at once, you can come with us."

They had just set off again, when Ducky Lucky saw Goosey Loosey.

"Oh, Goosey Loosey," he quacked, "the sky in the woods is falling down. We have to tell the king right away! You can come with us."

So the four birds went along, until they met Foxy Loxy.

"Good day to you all!" said the

crafty fox. "Where are you going this fine day?"

"We're off to see the king," announced Chicken Licken. "The sky fell on my head in the woods. We must tell him at once."

Foxy Loxy grinned slyly. "I can show you a short cut," he said, leading the way.

So the four birds followed Foxy Loxy, until they came to a narrow, dark hole in the hillside.

"This way!" said sly Foxy Loxy. He led Cocky Locky, Ducky Lucky and Goosey Loosey into his den. Chicken Licken was about to follow when… all of a sudden, Goosey Loosey let out a loud "Honk!" Then Ducky Lucky let out a shrill "Quack!" and Cocky Locky cried out, "Cock-a-doodle-do!"

"Foxy Loxy has eaten Goosey Loosey, Ducky Lucky, and Cocky Locky," cried Chicken Licken. "I must run away!"

Chicken Licken ran all the way home without stopping. And she never did tell the king that the sky was falling down.

The Big Ship Sails

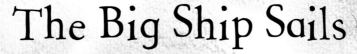

The big ship sails on the ally-ally-oh,
The ally-ally-oh, the ally-ally-oh.
Oh, the big ship sails on the ally-ally-oh
On the last day of September.

The captain said it will never, never do,
Never, never do, never, never do.
The captain said it will never, never do
On the last day of September.

The big ship sank to the bottom of the sea,
The bottom of the sea, the bottom of the sea.
The big ship sank to the bottom of the sea
On the last day of September.

We all dip our heads in the deep blue sea,
The deep blue sea, the deep blue sea.
We all dip our heads in the deep blue sea
On the last day of September.

Here We Go Round

Here we go round the mulberry bush,
The mulberry bush, the mulberry bush.
Here we go round the mulberry bush,
On a cold and frosty morning.

This is the way we wash our clothes,
Wash our clothes, wash our clothes.
This is the way we wash our clothes,
On a cold and frosty morning.

This is the way we iron our clothes,
Iron our clothes, iron our clothes.
This is the way we iron our clothes,
On a cold and frosty morning.

Head in the Clouds

How high can I go, does anyone know?
Perhaps to the top of the trees.
And if I do, well I wonder (don't you?)
What I'll see when I'm flying so free?

A giraffe has a neck that is so very tall,
It can stretch up incredibly high,
It can take a good look over many a wall,
And I wonder, oh why can't I?

Here on my swing I can see all around,
Over the whole neighbourhood.
But all of a sudden, I start going down,
Just as the view's getting good!

Little Bonnie Blue

Little Bonnie Blue, out in the meadow,
Smelling the flowers so sweet.
She will pick a few of the flowers that grow
And prettily bloom at her feet.

Colours shimmer soft, heavy under dew,
Waiting for the sun to climb.
Bonnie Blue will watch, as the flowers lift
Their heads towards sunshine.

Wherever you wander, Little Bonnie Blue,
You will walk on a carpet so sweet,
Made from meadow flowers, in every kind of hue,
Spread softly beneath your feet.

One, Two, Buckle my Shoe

One, two, buckle my shoe;

Three, four, knock at the door;

Five, six, pick up sticks;

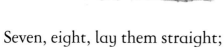

Seven, eight, lay them straight;

Nine, ten, a big fat hen;

Eleven, twelve, dig and delve;

Thirteen, fourteen, maids a-courting;

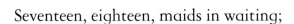

Fifteen, sixteen, maids in the kitchen;

Seventeen, eighteen, maids in waiting;

Nineteen, twenty, my plate's empty!

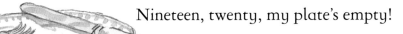

Our Home is a Castle!

Some people live in bungalows,
Without stairs to climb.
And some live way up in the clouds –
That must be sublime!

A man we know lives in a boat
And sails to where he pleases.
You can build a house with ice,
If all around you freezes!

But no one else has got a home
As wonderful as ours –
We live in a castle with a
Turret and some towers!

We can eat delicious food
In our banquet hall.
And when we're in a party mood,
We host a fancy ball!

The Washing Line!

My clothes are hanging on the line
So colourful and free,
They look like party bunting –
Hung up for all to see!

Red, blue, pink, yellow and green,
The colours are so bright,
They might be birds of paradise
Ready to take flight.

Some people don't like washing,
They look at me and ask:
How can you be so jolly about
Such a loathsome task?

To some it may seem like a chore
To wash and scrub and clean,
But I like nothing better than
My washing daydreams!

Visiting a Friend!

I'm going on a visit, to see my best friend, Grace.
She lives across the meadow in a very pretty place.
She hasn't got a ceiling, four walls or a door,
In fact she doesn't really even have a proper floor!

On my way I'll gather pretty flowers that I see,
To give to my friend Grace when I visit her for tea.
It's not an ordinary tea; she doesn't like cream cake,
She really much prefers to eat the flowers that I take!

She lives out in the open, beneath the sky, so blue.
She has four legs and a tail – have you figured out my clue?
Grace is not a human friend. She doesn't go to school.
Well of course she doesn't – ponies *don't* go, as a rule!

Yawning!

The strangest, funny feeling is creeping over me;
It makes me feel all stretchy, whatever can it be?
It's rising through my body; I cannot keep it in,
My arms are stretching upwards and my mouth is opening…

Yawn… oh my goodness! **Yawn**… Oh, how strange!
My mouth is like a cavern on a mountain range.
Yawn… I can't stop it! **Yawn**… there it goes!
And if I try to close my mouth it comes out through my nose!

Yawn… well I never! **Yawn**… oh my, oh me!
I'm making such a strange noise, like a foghorn out at sea!
Yawn… I think it's catching! **Yawn**… it's your turn now.
Is there a way to stop a yawn? I wish you'd tell me how!

Pussycat Mole

Pussycat Mole jumped over a coal,
And in her best petticoat burnt a great hole.
Pussycat's weeping; she'll have no more milk,
Until her best petticoat's mended with silk.

Frisky Lamb

A frisky lamb and a frisky child
Playing their pranks in a cowslip meadow:
The sky all blue and the air all mild
And the fields all sun and the lanes half-shadow.

On the Grassy Banks

On the grassy banks
Lambkins at their pranks;
Woolly sisters, woolly brothers,
Jumping off their feet,
While their woolly mothers
Watch them and bleat.

Pussycat Sits by the Fire

Pussycat sits by the fire.
How did she come there?
In walks the little dog,
Says, "Pussycat! Are you there?
How do you do, Mistress Pussycat?
Mistress Pussycat, how d'ye do?"
"I thanks you kindly, little dog,
I fare as well as you!"

Tiggy-Touchwood

Tiggy-tiggy-touchwood, my fine hen,
She lays an egg each day.
Tiggy-tiggy-touchwood, my black hen,
I never will send her away!

Mrs Hen

Chook, chook, chook, chook, chook,
Good morning, Mrs Hen.
How many chickens have you got?
Madam, I've got ten.
Four of them are yellow,
And four of them are brown,
And two of them are speckled red,
The nicest in the town.

Bless You

Bless you, bless you, burnie-bee,
Tell me when my wedding be;
If it be tomorrow day,
Take your wings and fly away.
Fly to the east, fly to the west,
Fly to him I love the best.

A Rat

There was a rat,
For want of stairs,
Went down a rope
To say his prayers.

Milking

Cushy cow, bonny, let down thy milk,
And I will give thee a gown of silk;
A gown of silk and a silver tree,
If thou wilt let down thy milk for me.

Punctuality

Be always on time,
Too late is a crime.

Parliament Soldiers

High diddle ding, did you hear the bells ring?
The parliament soldiers are gone to the king.
Some they did laugh, and some they did cry
To see the parliament soldiers go by.

Ride Away

Ride away, ride away, Johnny shall ride,
He shall have a pussycat tied to one side;
He shall have a little dog tied to the other,
And Johnny shall ride to see his grandmother.

The Lucky Shoes

Today was a very special day. Sophie and Gemma, were going to perform in their first ever ballet concert. All of their friends and family would be in the audience watching them dance.

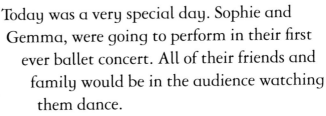

"I hope we don't make any mistakes," said Sophie, who was feeling nervous.

"I'll be wearing my lucky ballet shoes," said Gemma, "and they haven't let me down yet!"

The two friends walked to the concert together. They **skipped** happily through the park, twirling and leaping as they went. It was a hot day and, as they had plenty of time, they stopped for a while to catch their breath and drink some water.

"Phew, I'm so hot," gasped Gemma. "I think I'll take off my shoes for a while." As the two girls sat there resting and chatting, they didn't notice a little puppy sneaking up on them and running off with Gemma's lucky shoes. When Sophie and Gemma got up to go, Gemma couldn't find her shoes anywhere.

"My lucky shoes!" she gasped. "Where are they?"

Sophie and Gemma searched beneath bushes and under trees, but there was no trace of Gemma's lucky shoes.

Meanwhile, another little dancer was also making her way through the park to the ballet concert. She saw Gemma's lucky shoes on the path where the puppy had dropped them, and picked them up.

"Oh! What lovely shoes. Somebody must have dropped them," she thought. And wondering if they would fit her, she took her own shoes off to try them on. But the little dancer's head was so full of dreams about dancing in the lovely shoes, that she didn't notice the little puppy bound out from behind some bushes and run away with her shoes – and Gemma's lucky shoes as well! The little dancer was sitting on the path feeling very puzzled when Sophie ran up to her.

"Oh, hello," she said. "Have you seen a lovely pair of ballet shoes anywhere? They belong to my friend Gemma and they're her lucky shoes. They just disappeared!"

"Yes," replied the little dancer. "They were right here, but now they've gone. My own shoes have vanished, too!"

"How strange!" said

Sophie, scratching her head.

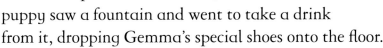

While Sophie and Gemma continued to search for the lucky shoes, the **cheeky** little puppy was having a lovely time scampering around the park. After a while, the puppy saw a fountain and went to take a drink from it, dropping Gemma's special shoes onto the floor.

Before long, another little girl came along and found the dainty ballet shoes.

"How pretty!" exclaimed the girl as she put them on and danced around the fountain. Feeling very lucky to have found such pretty shoes, she was about to run off to show her mother. But just then, Sophie and Gemma's friend, Jessica, happened to come past, also on her way to the concert. She saw the little girl dancing around and recognized Gemma's special shoes right away.

"Excuse me," she said to the little girl, "but are those your shoes? They look just like a pair that belong to my friend Gemma."

"No," replied the girl, "they're not mine. I just found them on the floor." The little girl took the shoes off and gave them to Jessica.

"They are lovely shoes," she said. "I hope your friend won't mind that I tried them on."

"I'm sure she'll be so pleased to get them back that she won't mind at all," said Jessica. "I'm just going to watch her dance in a concert. Perhaps you'd like to come and see her dance, too."

"Oh, yes," replied the girl, and she ran off to ask her mum.

The two girls went off to the concert together, and on the way they met Sophie and Gemma. They had found the ballet shoes belonging to the other little dancer, but were still searching for Gemma's lucky shoes.

"My lucky shoes!" cried Gemma when she saw what Jessica was carrying. "Thank goodness you found them."

They all hurried off to the concert hall and got there just in time for Sophie and Gemma to change for the performance.

Gemma and Sophie both danced beautifully, without making a single mistake.

As Gemma and Sophie took their final bow, the sound of rapturous applause rang in their ears.

"Your shoes really are lucky," smiled Sophie. "They went dancing all around the park this morning, but they still found their way back to you!"

"Yes," replied Gemma. "I always knew these shoes were rather special. I'll never let them out of my sight again!"

The Three Billy Goats Gruff

Once upon a time, there were three Billy Goats Gruff. There was a little billy goat with little horns. There was a middle-sized billy goat with middle-sized horns. And there was a big billy goat with very big horns.

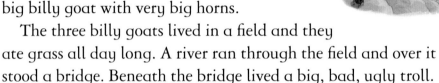

The three billy goats lived in a field and they ate grass all day long. A river ran through the field and over it stood a bridge. Beneath the bridge lived a big, bad, ugly troll.

One day, the little billy goat looked at the field over the bridge. The grass looked long and juicy. He wanted to eat that grass. So the brave little billy goat went onto the bridge with a **trip trap, trip trap.** But the bad troll jumped out.

"I'm going to eat you!" he said.

"No, you can't eat me!" said the little billy goat. "I'm just a little goat. Wait for the middle-sized goat and eat him. He will be far more tasty."

So the bad troll did just that. Then the middle-sized billy goat looked at the field over the bridge. The grass looked long and juicy. He wanted to eat that grass.

So the middle-sized billy goat went onto the bridge with a

clip clop, clip clop. But the bad troll jumped out.

"I'm going to eat you!" he said.

"No, you can't eat me!" said the middle-sized billy goat.

"I'm just a middle-sized goat. Wait for the big goat and eat him." So the bad troll did just that.

Then the big billy goat looked at the field over the bridge. The grass looked long and juicy. He wanted to eat that grass.

So the big billy goat went onto the bridge with a thump, thump, thump, thump. But the bad troll jumped out.

"I'm going to eat you!" he said.

"No, you can't eat me," said the big billy goat. "I'm a big goat and I have very big horns. I will toss you into the air with my big horns." He put his head down and ran at the bad troll. He tossed him high up into the air. Then the bad troll fell into the river. And that was the end of him!

Fingers and Toes

These are my fingers and these are my toes.
This is my head and this is my nose.
These are my ears, on my head at the side.
These are my eyes, I can open them wide.

This is my mouth and here are my teeth.
These are my knees and my feet are beneath.
I can wave my arms and wiggle my nose.
I can stretch my arms and touch my toes.

I can clap my hands together, and then. . .
It's time to start all over again!

My Dog, Blue

My dog, Blue, is soft to touch –
I love to cuddle him so much.
His ears droop down in a cute way,
His tail can wag as if to say:

Cuddle me!

My dog, Blue, is my best friend,
So please don't ask me if I'll lend
My dog to you, the answer's no –
I take him everywhere I go...

... and cuddle him!

When it's time to go to bed,
I snuggle up and rest my head.
I love to be alone with Blue,
I'm sure you know just what I do...

... I cuddle him!

The Owl and the Pussy Cat

The Owl and the Pussy Cat went to sea
In a beautiful pea-green boat,
They took some honey, and plenty of money,
Wrapped up in a five pound note.
The Owl looked up to the stars above,
And sang to a small guitar,
"Oh lovely Pussy! Oh Pussy, my love,
What a beautiful Pussy you are, you are, you are,
What a beautiful Pussy you are."

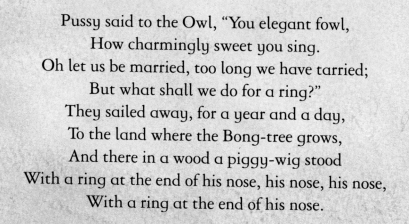

Pussy said to the Owl, "You elegant fowl,
How charmingly sweet you sing.
Oh let us be married, too long we have tarried;
But what shall we do for a ring?"
They sailed away, for a year and a day,
To the land where the Bong-tree grows,
And there in a wood a piggy-wig stood
With a ring at the end of his nose, his nose, his nose,
With a ring at the end of his nose.

Jack Frost

The stars are out, the night is clear,
It's freezing cold – **Jack Frost is here!**
He points his finger at a tree,
And freezes it quite easily.

Tomorrow, you'll awake to find
The things Jack Frost has left behind:
A frozen pond, an icy lane
And patterns on a window pane.

He's made the green grass icy white;
The frozen crystals shine so bright.
This cold and frosty winter scene,
Means just one thing –
Jack Frost has been!

The Goose-Girl

A princess, who was to marry a prince, set off on a journey to her wedding day with her maid. She took precious gifts for her new husband, and wore fine clothes for the wedding.

The maid, however, was an evil girl. She made the princess swap clothes with her and give her all the treasures.

When they arrived at the palace, the prince mistook the maid for his bride and the princess for a maid.

"Put my maid to work with the geese," said the wicked imposter.

But the old king could not help but notice how beautiful the new goose-girl was, and asked her where she had come from. The poor girl didn't tell the king, for she had promised not to tell a soul.

"If you can't tell me, then tell the stove," said the wise old king, and he left the room and hid by the boiler pipe where he could hear her. The real princess sobbed as she told the stove the truth about who she was. The old king heard everything.

The wicked maid was banished, and the true princess married her prince and lived happily ever after.

Bed in Summer

In winter I get up at night,
And dress by yellow candle-light.
In summer, quite the other way,
I have to go to bed by day.

Bedtime

The evening is coming; the sun sinks to rest,
The rooks are all flying straight home to nest.
"Caw!" says the rook, as he flies overhead;
"It's time little people were going to bed!"

The Owl

When cats run home and light is come,
And dew is cold upon the ground,
And the far-off stream is dumb
And the whirring sail goes round;
Alone and warming his five wits,
The white owl in the belfry sits.

The Wise Old Owl

There was an old owl who lived in an oak;
The more he heard the less he spoke.
The less he spoke, the more he heard.
Why aren't we like that wise old bird?

Brahms Lullaby

Lullaby, and good night,
With rosy bed light,
With lilies overspread,
Is my sweet baby's bed.

Lullaby, and good night,
You're your mother's delight,
Shining angels beside,
My darling abide.

Little Fred

When little Fred went to bed,
He always said his prayers;
He kissed Mama, and then Papa,
And straightaway went upstairs.

The Tortoise and the Hare

Once upon a time, there was a hare who was always boasting about how fast he was.

"I," he would say, puffing out his chest and flexing his legs, "am the speediest animal in the forest. I have never been beaten. I challenge anyone to try and beat me."

And, of course, nobody took up the challenge because he was right – he was the fastest animal in the forest.

The animals who lived in the forest were becoming tired of Hare's bragging, until one day, much to everyone's surprise, after Hare had been boasting even more than normal.

"Okay, Hare. I'll race you," Tortoise said.

"Whaaaaat?" laughed Hare. "You've got to be joking. Tortoise, you're the slowest animal in the forest. I'll run circles around you."

"You might be fast," replied Tortoise, "but speed isn't everything. Why don't we have a race? You can

keep your boasting until you actually beat me."

"Speed might not be everything but it sure helps in a race," laughed Hare. He laughed so much that he fell to his knees and thumped the floor with his fist. He'd never heard of anything so ridiculous in his life.

That night, while the forest animals prepared the course, Tortoise went to bed early so he'd have a lot of energy for the race. Hare, meanwhile, stayed up late boxing with his friends. He knew he could beat the slow tortoise even if he was tired.

There was a buzz of **excitement** in the forest the next morning. No one had heard of Hare ever losing a race so this was going to be quite an event to watch! Everyone gathered at the starting line to watch the race begin. All the forest animals wanted Tortoise to win, but deep down they knew that Hare was the fastest.

Tortoise was already at the starting line, trying his best to look confident. He looked around for Hare, who had just arrived and was making his way to the starting line. He strutted towards Tortoise with his chest puffed out proudly. The crowd fell silent…

"On your marks, get set…GO!" cried the starting fox.

And Hare flew off at high speed, leaving a cloud of dust where he had just stood. The tortoise trudged behind much, much, much more slooooowly.

Hare decided to take a quick look behind to see where the slow tortoise was. When he saw that Tortoise was far, far away, he decided to stop for breakfast. He feasted on some juicy carrots. Then he lay on his back, fiddled with his ears, and yawned.

"This is just too easy," he said, loud enough for just about all the animals in the forest to hear. "I think I'll have forty winks and catch up with him later." Soon he was snoring happily away. ZZZZZZZZ!

Tortoise got to where Hare was lying, fast asleep. "Maybe I should wake him?" he thought, as he plodded past Hare. "No, I'm sure Hare wouldn't like that. He will wake up soon enough and come whizzing by."

And so Tortoise plodded on and on and on. Hare slept, on and on and on. In Hare's dreams, all the forest animals cheered and clapped as he streamed past the finish line.

The sun began to sink, and still Tortoise plodded on, and still Hare slept. The sun was just about to set when Hare awoke with a jolt.

He could just see Tortoise in the distance, plodding slowly

and carefully towards the finish line.

"Noooooooo!" cried Hare. He leapt to his feet and charged towards the finish.

He ran as fast as his legs could carry him, but it just wasn't fast enough – he was too late!

Tortoise was over the line before him. Hare had been beaten fair and square.

Tortoise was a hero, and all the forest animals were there to cheer him.

After that, if anyone heard Hare boasting about how fast he could run, they reminded him about the day that Tortoise had beaten him.

"Slow and steady won the race," they would say.

And all Hare could do was smile and shrug because, after all, they were absolutely right.

Things I Wear

When it's cold I wrap up warm,
In a scarf and mittens.
Pyjamas are for bedtime
When I snuggle like a kitten.

Sometimes I like to dress up
In fancy things to wear;
A pretty velvet party dress
And sparkles in my hair.

But what I like much better,
Than glamour, glitz and glory,
Is to dress up as a heroine
From some romantic story!

Wallflower

The music is playing, the dancers are spinning
Around and around to a waltz, and they're grinning.
So happy they look as they take to the floor,
When each dance has finished, they all ask for more.

But one pretty lady stands all by herself
With her back to the wall, is she left on the shelf?
Her ball gown is lovely, her hair looks a treat,
Will nobody dance with this wallflower so sweet?

Someone approaches, a handsome young man!
As he greets her he bows just as low as he can.
May I have the honour of dancing with you?
Now she's happily dancing and no longer blue!

Party Time in Twinkle Town

The fairies of Twinkle Town were excited because they were expecting a very special visitor. Only the town's chief fairy knew who was coming, and she was keeping it a closely guarded secret.

"You'll just have to wait and see," she teased, when the little fairies begged her to tell them.

Everyone was hard at work using their magic to clean and tidy. Even the flowers were getting a dust and a polish!

Soon everything was ready for the surprise visitor, and the fairies of Twinkle Town didn't have to wait long before they heard a **magical tinkling sound** getting louder and

louder, and a beautiful pink mist getting
closer and closer. Finally, there was a gentle
explosion of lights and colour, and then their
eyes met with a wonderful sight...

It was the Fairy Queen!
Everyone clapped and cheered.

The Fairy Queen admired Twinkle
Town and declared it the cleanest town
in Fairyland. The party food was
fantastic; the cakes were magic and
when you bit into them little birds
flew out and began to sing.

The Queen was very
impressed. "Goodness me!" she
exclaimed. "All this must have taken a lot of
hard work and magic."

"Let's have some dancing," suggested the chief fairy. She
raised her magic wand to conjure up some fairy dance music...
but nothing happened.

"Whoops!" she said, blushing slightly. "I'll just try that
again." But still nothing happened!

"Oh dear," said the Fairy Queen. "You must have used up
all your magic dust getting ready for my party!"

The Fairy Queen waved her own special magic wand and
conjured up some music. The dancing went on way into
the night, and everyone agreed it was the best
party that Twinkle Town had ever had.

One for Sorrow

One for sorrow,
Two for joy,
Three for a girl,
Four for a boy,
Five for silver,
Six for gold,
Seven for a secret
Never to be told.

Tinker, Tailor, Soldier, Sailor

Tinker,

Tailor,

Soldier,

Sailor,

Rich man,

Poor man,

Beggarman,

Thief!

Woodland Rescue

Bella loved nature. Whenever she went walking, she always looked out for wildlife and trees.

One day, Bella was strolling through the woods. As she walked along, she could hear the sounds of nature.

Chirp! Cheep! There were so many birds singing that it was hard to tell one from another. The different sounds blended together, creating a birdsong orchestra.

Just then, Bella heard something unusual.

Scraaaape! It was a scuttling and scraping. No animal that Bella knew of made a sound like that. Standing very still, Bella listened to hear where the sound was coming from. Slowly and quietly, so as not to scare the creature away, she peeped behind the nearest tree and there was a baby squirrel. It was scrambling to get out from a hollow at the bottom of the tree, but it was stuck.

Bella didn't want to frighten the poor creature, but she could see that it needed help. The squirrel had its paw stuck in a plastic drink bottle – so that's what was making the scraping sound!

The baby squirrel was frozen with fear as Bella bent down to release its trapped paw. When the paw was free, it still didn't move.

"Don't be frightened of me little squirrel, I'm here to help you," whispered Bella. But when the squirrel still didn't move, she crept away, back behind the tree, and waited as still as a statue. When the squirrel thought she'd gone, he scampered off to find his mother.

Bella was happy that she had rescued the squirrel, but she felt angry too.

"It's wrong to leave litter in the woods," she thought. And then Bella had a wonderful idea.

That evening, Bella invited her friends round for a sleepover.

"Bring some coloured crayons and pencils," she told them.

When her friends arrived, she told them all about her woodland rescue. Her friends all agreed to help.

Bella's parents were rather puzzled that Bella and her friends were so quiet that evening because sleepovers were usually much noisier than this!

"What are those girls up to?" asked Bella's dad. They soon found out that the girls had been working hard making a big poster to stick up at the entrance to the woods.

Litter Harms Wildlife, the poster read. It was decorated with beautiful pictures of squirrels, foxes, owls and lots of other woodland creatures.

Bella and her friends would make sure that everybody got the message.

Little Bear's Close Encounter

Little Bear looked up at the stars.

"I wish I was an astronaut," he sighed.

Little Bear dreamed of exploring the world outside the window. He liked living in Emma's bedroom, but he sometimes wondered what it would be like to climb a mountain or go deep-sea diving. Most of all, Little Bear longed to meet an alien.

"Twinkle, twinkle, little bear," he sang to himself. "How I wonder what's up there."

"What are you looking at?" asked Monkey, coming over to join him at the window.

"I'm looking for spaceships," replied Little Bear, pressing his furry nose up against the window. "I want to meet a real alien," he explained.

"I wonder what they look like?" said Monkey.

Little Bear told Monkey that Emma had a book all about aliens that they read together.

"They come in all shapes and sizes," he said.

"Are they scary?" asked Monkey.

"I hope not!" Little Bear replied.

Suddenly a big black shape appeared at the window, looming over the two friends.

"Aaargh! An alien!" cried Little Bear, jumping down from the windowsill.

"Do aliens meow?" asked Monkey.

"I'm not sure that they do," whispered Little Bear, peeping out from between his paws.

"Do aliens purr?" asked Monkey.

"It didn't say anything about purring in Emma's book," said Little Bear, feeling a little braver.

Do aliens have whiskers and a long furry tail?" giggled Monkey.

"Definitely not!" said Little Bear, beginning to feel rather foolish.

Little Bear and Monkey climbed back onto the windowsill. Was it an alien? No it was Emma's cat, Sooty.

"Meow!" said Sooty.

Little Bear decided that he'd had enough excitement for one night.

"Perhaps I don't want to meet an alien, after all," he chuckled.

Princess Mia and the Big Smile

Princess Mia was a very lively girl. She was always bouncing around and getting into scrapes. Her father wanted her to act more like a princess.

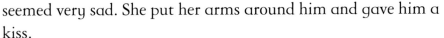

"You must be more serious!" the king told his daughter.

The Princess looked at the king's serious face. An then she looked at his down-turned mouth. He looked so serious that he seemed very sad. She put her arms around him and gave him a kiss.

"It's not me who needs to be more serious," she told her dad. "It's you who needs to smile more, Daddy."

Princess Mia showed the king how to dance around the palace gardens and do cartwheels. **Whee!** The king wasn't very good at them but he kept trying again and again.

Suddenly, his face wasn't quite so serious. Princess Mia showed the king how to make a kite swoop through the sky like a bird. **Whoosh!**

The king got his string tangled once or twice, but he did quite well for a beginner.

His face was looking less serious by the minute.

"Well done, Daddy!" cried Princess Mia. The king's mouth twitched. It started to turn up at the corners. Then he gave a beautifully big smile.

"I had forgotten about cartwheels and flying kites!" he said with glee. "I thought that they were a waste of time!"

"Silly Daddy!" said Princess Mia.

The king did a cartwheel and bounced onto his throne to pass some laws.

"From now on," said the king, "I decree that everyone **must** do at least ten cartwheels a day! We will teach silliness in schools! And everyone in the palace will have one hour off a day to practise kite flying!"

The king gave Princess Mia a beautiful charm necklace.

"This will remind you that everyone needs a little bit of silliness to keep them smiling," he said.

"Silly Daddy," said Princess Mia. "I've always known that!" And she danced out of the palace to play.

The Little Turtle Dove

High in the pine tree,
The little turtle dove
Made a little nursery
To please her little love.
"Coo," said the turtle dove,
"Coo," said she;
In the long, shady branches
Of the dark pine tree.

Bow Wow

Bow, wow, says the dog,
Meow, meow, says the cat,
Grunt, grunt, says the hog,
And squeak goes the rat.
Tu-whoo, says the owl,
Cau, cau, says the crow,
Quack, quack, says the duck,
And what cuckoos say, you know!

See a Pin

See a pin and pick it up,
All the day you'll have good luck;
See a pin and let it lay,
Bad luck you'll have all the day!

Mr Nobody

Mr Nobody is a nice young man,
He comes to the door with his hat in his hand.
Down she comes all dressed in silk,
A rose in her bosom, as white as milk.
She takes off her gloves, she shows me her ring,
Tomorrow, tomorrow, the wedding begins.

Oliver Twist

Oliver Twist
You can't do this,
So what's the use of trying?
Touch your toe,
Touch your knee,
Clap your hands,
Away we go.

Old Pudding-Pie Woman

There was an old woman
Sold pudding and pies;
She went to the mill
And dust blew in her eyes.
Hot puddings, and cold puddings,
And nice pies to sell;
Wherever she goes, if you have a good nose,
You may follow her by the smell.

Let's Play, Baby

One little baby, wide awake and bouncy.
What does he want to do?
Let's play . . .peek-a-boo!
One happy baby, halfway through his breakfast.
What does he want to do?
Let's play... peek-a-boo!
One friendly baby, ready to get dressed.
But what does he want to do?
Let's play... peek-a-boo!
One snuggly baby, ready for a story.
But what does he want to do?
Let's play... peek-a-boo!
One sleepy baby, tucked in, warm and cozy.
But what does he want to do?
Let's play... peek-a-boo!
One sleepy baby, ready for his bed.
But what does he do instead?
He plays... peek-a-boo!

356

Night-Night, Baby

The flowers are feeling sleepy,
Blue spotty dog is, too.
Time for them to say night-night...
What about you?

Cuddle up, so warm and snug,
It's time for your bedtime, too!
The sun has slipped away to sleep...
What about you?

The moon is shining in the sky,
The stars are peeping through.
All around is calm and quiet
And now you're sleeping, too!

Ten in the Bed

There were ten in the bed and the little one said,
"Roll over, roll over."

So they all rolled over and one fell out.
There were nine in the bed and the little one said,
"Roll over, roll over."

So they all rolled over and one fell out.
There were eight in the bed and the little one said,
"Roll over, roll over."

So they all rolled over and one fell out.
There were seven in the bed and the little one said,
"Roll over, roll over."

So they all rolled over and one fell out.
There were six in the bed and the little one said,
"Roll over, roll over."

So they all rolled over and one fell out.
There were five in the bed and the little one said,
"Roll over, roll over."

So they all rolled over and one fell out.
There were four in the bed and the little one said,
"Roll over, roll over."

So they all rolled over and one fell out.
There were three in the bed and the little one said,
"Roll over, roll over."

So they all rolled over and one fell out.
There were two in the bed and the little one said,
"Roll over, roll over."

So they all rolled over and one fell out.
There was one in the bed and the little one said,
"Goodnight!"

Hansel and Gretel

Hansel and Gretel lived by the forest with their father, a poor woodcutter, and their stepmother.

One evening, the family had nothing left to eat but a few crusts of bread. Hansel and Gretel went to bed hungry. As they lay in their beds, they heard the grown-ups talking.

"There are too many mouths to feed," said their stepmother. "We must take your children into the forest and leave them there."

"Never!" cried their father.

But the next morning, Hansel and Gretel's stepmother woke them early.

"Get up!" she ordered. "We're going into the forest to chop wood."

She handed them each a crust of bread for their lunch.

Hansel broke his bread into tiny pieces in his pocket, and as they walked, he secretly dropped a trail of crumbs on the ground.

Deep in the forest, Hansel and Gretel's father built them a fire.

"We are going to chop wood now," he said. "We'll return at sunset."

After a while, the children shared Gretel's bread, and then they curled up at the foot of an old oak tree and fell asleep.

When Hansel and Gretel woke up, they looked for the trail of breadcrumbs, but they were gone! The forest birds had eaten them.

"We'll wait till morning," Hansel said. "Then we can find our way home."

The next morning, the children walked through the forest, until they came to a little house – made of gingerbread! The roof was dripping with sugary icing, the door was made of candy canes and the garden was filled with colourful lollipops.

Delighted, the hungry children began to feast upon the sweets. As they ate, an old woman hobbled out of the house.

"You must be starving, my dears," she said. "Come inside and have a proper meal."

The old woman fed them well and then put them to bed. But Hansel and Gretel didn't know that the kind old woman was really a wicked witch. As she watched them sleep, she cackled, "I'll soon fatten these two up. Then they will make a proper meal for me!"

The following morning, the witch dragged Hansel from his bed, and threw him into a cage. Then she made Gretel cook her brother a big breakfast.

"Your brother is too skinny," the witch told Gretel. "I'll keep him locked up until he is nice and plump – and then I'll eat him up!"

Over the next few days, Hansel had as much food as he could eat. And every morning, the witch made him stick out his finger so she could feel whether he was fat enough to eat.

But Hansel knew that the old witch could hardly see, so he stuck a chicken bone through the cage instead.

"Still too scrawny," the witch would say.

One day the witch got tired of waiting and decided to eat Hansel right away.

"Light the oven!" the witch ordered Gretel. "Now crawl in and see if it's hot enough."

Gretel knew the witch was planning to cook her as well. So she decided to trick the witch.

"The oven's much too small for me," she said.

"Nincompoop!" cried the witch. "Even I could get into that oven. Look!" And she stuck her head inside.

With a great big shove, Gretel pushed the witch into the oven and slammed the door shut.

Gretel freed Hansel from his cage, and they danced happily around the kitchen. "We're safe! We're safe!" they sang. When the children looked around the witch's house, they found chests crammed with gold and sparkling jewels. They filled their pockets and set off for home.

They seemed to find their way straight home, where their delighted father greeted them with hugs and kisses.

He told them that their cruel stepmother had died, so they had nothing to fear. Hansel and Gretel showed him the treasure they had found.

"We will never go hungry again!" they said. They all lived happily ever after.

Wee Willie Winkie

Wee Willie Winkie
Runs through the town,
Upstairs and downstairs
In his nightgown.

Rapping at the window,
Crying through the lock,
Are all the children in their beds?
For now it's eight o'clock.

Boys and Girls Come Out to Play

Boys and girls come out to play,
The moon doth shine as bright as day!
Leave your supper and leave your sleep,
And join your playfellows in the street.
Come with a whoop and come with a call,
Come with a good will or not at all.

Go to Bed First

Go to bed first,
A golden purse;
Go to bed second,
A golden pheasant;
Go to bed third,
A golden bird.

Go to Bed Late

Go to bed late,
Stay very small;
Go to bed early,
Grow very tall.

Go to Bed, Tom

Go to bed, Tom,
Go to bed, Tom,
Tired or not, Tom,
Go to bed, Tom.

Bye, Baby Bunting

Bye, baby bunting,
Daddy's gone a-hunting,
Gone to get a rabbit-skin,
To wrap my baby bunting in.

Now the Day is Over

Now the day is over,
Night is drawing nigh,
Shadows of the evening
Steal across the sky.

Now the darkness gathers,
Stars begins to peep,
Birds and beasts and flowers
Soon will be asleep.

Come to Bed, Says Sleepy-Head

"Come to bed," says Sleepy-head;
"Tarry a while," says Slow;
"Put on the pot," says Greedy-gut,
"Let's sup before we go."

Golden Slumbers

Golden slumbers kiss your eyes,
Smiles await you when you rise;
Sleep, pretty baby, do not cry,
And I will sing you a lullaby.

Star Light, Star Bright

Star light, star bright,
First star I see tonight,
I wish I may, I wish I might,
Have the wish I wish tonight.

Hush, My Little One

Hush, my little one
When the day is done.
You must go to sleep,
The Lord your soul to keep.

How Many Miles to Babylon?

How many miles to Babylon?
Three score and ten.
Can I get there by candle-light?
Yes, and back again.
If your heels are nimble and light,
You may get there by candle-light.

Sleep Little Child

Sleep little child, go to sleep,
Mother is here by your bed.
Sleep little child, go to sleep,
Rest on the pillow your head.
The world is silent and still,
The moon shines bright on the hill,
Then creeps past the windowsill.
Sleep little child, go to sleep,
Oh sleep, go to sleep.

Five Little Ducks

Five little ducks went swimming one day,
Over the hills and far away.
Mother duck said, "Quack, quack, quack, quack,"
But only four little ducks came back.

Four little ducks went swimming one day,
Over the hills and far away.
Mother duck said, "Quack, quack, quack, quack,"
But only three little ducks came back.

Three little ducks went swimming one day,
Over the hills and far away.
Mother duck said, "Quack, quack, quack, quack,"
But only two little ducks came back.

Five Little Ducks

Two little ducks went swimming one day,
Over the hills and far away.
Mother duck said, "Quack, quack, quack, quack,"
But only one little duck came back.

One little duck went swimming one day,
Over the hills and far away.
Mother duck said, "Quack, quack, quack, quack,"
But none of the five little ducks came back.

Mother duck went swimming one day,
Over the hills and far away.
Mother duck said, "Quack, quack, quack, quack,"
And five little ducks came swimming back.

Puss in Boots

There was once an old miller who died, leaving his mill to his eldest son, his donkey to his middle son and his cat to his youngest son, who was called Jack. Jack was so poor that he could barely afford to feed himself, let alone the poor creature as well.

"What am I going to do with you?" Jack asked the cat.

Although he spoke to the cat, he certainly didn't expect an answer, so you can imagine his surprise when the cat said:

"Don't worry about a thing. Just give me a pair of boots, a hat and a sack and you'll soon discover what I'm worth."

Jack quickly saw that this was no ordinary puss, so with his last coins, he gave the cat what he wanted.

The cat looked so funny all dressed up that Jack laughed until his sides hurt. He decided to call him **Puss in Boots.**

The following morning Puss in Boots went hunting and immediately caught a fine rabbit. He set off to the king's palace with the rabbit in his sack. At the palace, he presented it to the king and said:

"This is a gift from my master, the Marquis of Carabas." (This was a name that he had just made up).

The king was delighted with the gift. "Perhaps I could call

on your master and thank him myself," he suggested.

Puss in Boots gave the king directions to his master's castle. The king promised he would call the next day, and bring his beautiful daughter, Melissa, with him.

The next morning, Puss in Boots took Jack to a lake on the road that he had told the king his master's castle was on. He told his master to get in the water, and as soon as Jack dived in, Puss in Boots hid his clothes and ran to meet the king.

"Help, help!" cried Puss, as soon as he spotted the king's carriage. "Robbers have stolen my master's clothes."

The king gave some spare clothes to Jack, who quickly got dressed. The king invited Jack to join him and Princess Melissa in the royal carriage. Jack looked so handsome that the princess fell in love with him on the spot.

Once they were all safely in the carriage, Puss in Boots raced ahead. He came to a field where some men were working.

"When the king comes passing by, you must tell him that these fields belong to the

Marquis of Carabas. If you don't, it'll be off with your heads!" he told the men.

Sure enough, when the king passed the field of workers he stopped and asked who owned the land.

"Why, the Marquis of Carabas, your Majesty," they all replied, for no one wanted to lose their head. The king was impressed, even though poor Jack looked a little confused.

As it happened, the fields and lands really belonged to a fierce giant who lived in a castle at the end of the road. Puss in Boots hurried to the castle and knocked on the door.

"WHO GOES THERE?" roared the giant.

"Just me," replied Puss in Boots. "I've travelled from far away because I've heard that you are a wonderful magician. I have heard that you can change yourself into any animal you want."

"True," said the giant, who was very vain and a bit of a show-off. Then he turned himself into a huge lion.

"That's very impressive," said Puss in Boots. "But I bet a huge fellow like you couldn't turn yourself into something small, such as... a teeny-tiny mouse!"

"Easy-peasy," boasted the giant, immediately turning himself into a little brown mouse. In a flash, the cunning puss pounced on the mouse and gobbled him up.

Just then, the king's carriage arrived at the castle. Puss in Boots raced out to welcome him.

"Welcome to the Marquis of Carabas's humble home," said the cat, with a sweeping bow.

"You mean to say that this is all yours?" said the king, turning to Jack. At first Jack looked confused, but when Puss in Boots winked at him, he held out his hand and led Princess Melissa into the castle.

The king was so impressed that when Jack, or the Marquis of Carabas as he was now called, asked him for his daughter's hand in marriage, he quickly agreed.

Indeed, he heartily congratulated himself on finding such a fine son-in-law. And from that day forth, the Marquis of Carabas, the princess, and, of course, Puss in Boots lived happily ever after.

Here is the Church

Here is the church,
Here is the steeple,
Look inside…
And see all the people!

The Cuckoo

Cuckoo, Cuckoo, what do you do?
In April I open my bill;
In May I sing night and day;
In June I change my tune;
In July, away I fly;
In August, away I must.

Jay-Bird

Jay-bird, jay-bird, sitting on a rail,
Picking his teeth with the end of his tail;
Mulberry leaves and calico sleeves –
All school teachers are hard to please.

I Hear Thunder

I hear thunder, I hear thunder,
Hark, don't you? Hark, don't you?
Pitter-patter raindrops,
Pitter-patter raindrops,
I'm wet through,
So are you.

Magpies

Black and white and white and black,
Beak and feathers, peck peck peck!
We love shiny, glittery things,
Don't let us near your diamond rings!

The Wheels on the Bus

The wheels on the bus go
Round and round,
Round and round,
Round and round.
The wheels on the bus go
Round and round,
All day long.

The wipers on the bus go
Swish, swish, swish!
Swish, swish, swish!
Swish, swish, swish!
The wipers on the bus go
Swish, swish, swish!
All day long.

The horn on the bus goes
Beep, beep, beep!
Beep, beep, beep!
Beep, beep, beep!
The horn on the bus goes
Beep, beep, beep!
All day long.

Five Little Monkeys

Five little monkeys jumping on the bed,
One fell off and bumped his head.
Mummy called the Doctor and the Doctor said,
"No more monkeys jumping on the bed!"

Four little monkeys jumping on the bed,
One fell off and bumped her head.
Mummy called the Doctor and the Doctor said,
"No more monkeys jumping on the bed!"

Three little monkeys jumping on the bed,
One fell off and bumped his head.
Mummy called the Doctor and the Doctor said,
"No more monkeys jumping on the bed!"

Five Little Monkeys

Two little monkeys jumping on the bed,
One fell off and bumped her head.
Mummy called the Doctor and the Doctor said,
"No more monkeys jumping on the bed!"

One little monkey jumping on the bed,
He fell off and bumped his head.
Mummy called the Doctor and the Doctor said,
"Put those monkeys straight to bed!"

Index

Index